Virgin Patiala Peg

Gaganjeet Gujral

Published by Gaganjeet Gujral, 2021.

VIRGIN PATIALA PEG

First edition. July 5, 2021.

Written by Gaganjeet Gujral.

I dedicate this book to my wife Tanya who has been of tremendous encouragement during witing this book, She was the one to ignite the spark inside of me to start writing. I dedicate this book to my professors and teachers who i took inspiration from, and who i admire tremendously. Prof Nitin Singh PhD, Shomu Sir, Sonu Sir. My fitness trainer Sivaraman. I dedicate the book to my parents, my father who supports me in my endeavours and my mother who is my freind everyday. I Dedicate this book to the Patiala Peg.

Patiala Peg is a Large measure of your prefered liquor of choice, made famous by His Royal Highness Bhupinder Singh of Patiala.

1.

Early Troubles.....

“I am back home” a feeble voice came from Karamjit as he quietly rushed himself closing the front door to his room, throwing away his school bag on the sofa, lurking in the corner of his room and laying down feeling like a sack of potatoes.

An immediate voice came from his uncle who was standing next to him waking up all his senses, “Have you received your test?”

Karamjit trembled up in fear and said stutteringly “T-T-T- Test?”

“Yes, the one that took place this morning” asked his uncle. Karamjit hesitatingly replied, “N-N-No, it was cancelled as the teacher felt sick & had to leave the classroom early on.”

“Now don’t waste your time lying up there like a pig in mud. Get up, eat your lunch and get back to study.” His uncle left the room without saying a further word and Karamjit slowly collecting himself from his couch rejuvenating his calmness, relieving himself thinking that his uncle hasn’t found that he has not attended his school from last five days.

He laid down on his back trying to get into the world of his own imagination at the same time hoping that he do not face any further trouble for the rest of the day. After some time, he fell asleep waking up in a new world giving him a strange nostalgic feeling of reality where he is travelling all around the world, exploring different countries, meeting with new people, tasting new dishes and influencing millions of lives around the globe with his persuasive communication skills & ability to inspire people.

Loosing count of time, he woke up late in the night only realizing it when he got a kick on his butt by his aunt. "You lazy thing you. Your uncle told you to study, no? And here you are, sleeping like you got no worries. Stand up, I said!" she shouted at the top of her voice.

He trembled up to the refrigerator to find something to eat and sat down on his study table to prepare for the test hoping he could get something imprinted on his mind.

It was however not an unusual day for Karamjit Singh, a seventeen year old Sikh boy who was the only son of his father living in the Patiala district of Punjab with his uncle and aunt. He was five feet eight inches tall weighing roughly hundred and twenty-five pounds. He lived with his uncle and aunt alone. Their house was located in an alley passing from the main Sirhind Road. His father, Balkar Singh who was a Captain in the Indian Army was deployed most of the times at different posts almost all the year & had no luxury time to spend with his only son. His mother, Kulvir Kaur died in a car accident when he was just seven. He grew up with his uncle Colonel Gurtej Singh who was now retired personnel from the military.

Living up without parents in his uncle's presence who was a strict and disciplined person having complete authority over the choices of Karamjit made him an introvert, insecure and unconfident boy who was just into himself. And his aunt, Jaswinder Kaur left him no chance to enjoy his teen life keeping him in a lot of troubles which even led to him being beaten up by his uncle without any of his fault.

One day, while she was cleaning the floor, she accidently bumped into an expensive flower vase that his uncle Gurtej Singh had bought from Japan. When Gurtej Singh entered the room, she put the whole blame on Karamjit realizing the anguish that she would have to face from Gurtej Singh. And consequently, Karamjit got punished by his uncle for breaking the pot that he didn't even touched. Gurtej Singh, however was different than his wife Jaswinder Kaur. He always took his decisions which would benefit Karamjit but he was rude which was a direct consequence according to many because he served in the Indian Army for so many years which made him strict and disciplined. So he never refrained from using the rod to use as a punishment for Karamjit to make him realize his mistakes and then never to have him repeat them again.

He would take Karamjit to morning running and leave him gasping for breath after making him run for more than five miles daily. Karamjit however, hated doing any physical exercises but it didn't mattered what he liked or disliked, he had to do it because it was an order from his uncle that was supreme for him even though he hated it. He never liked to eat groceries too but again, he would not only drink the stuff he didn't liked but also drank some of the worst tasting juices from raw vegetables which they prepared at home in their garden.

Jaswinder Kaur on the other hand was completely different as she never considered Karamjit her nephew and always found ways in which she could do some harm to him and make his life worse than ever before. Karamjit although was afraid of social associations because of living under a constrained environment offering him little to no freedom, he had keen interest in travelling and a sense of curiosity to explore new places perhaps because of the constipated desire that built inside him living in an environment of social conformity offering little attention to his own identity.

Karamjit's day usually started with him going to his school. He was not one of the kind who was pursuing his passion which was deeply suppressed and one of the reasons which contributed to it was that he was put into a convent school since he was a child which also led him to form his religious beliefs in Sikhism and shaped his mentality and thought process in a significant way.

He had few friends and even those who were his friends usually abstained from communicating with him. That was partly because of the fact that he was considered a different kid with unusual perspective of looking at the world. So, every time he tried to speak and present his world view, his views were generally unwelcomed and not accepted. This led him to forming a belief that the world is a strange place to live, and he is someone who is distinguished from the rest because of his different conceptions about life. It first started with his teachers who told him that he was mentally retarded, lacked the intellectual faculty to comprehend the information just like other kids and couldn't compete at the same level as the rest of them when he was very young.

And later on, his aunt did her part by not embracing and encouraging Karamjit's abilities that he could improve himself in terms of his intellect. The result was that Karamjit had no sense of significance and worth for himself and his abilities to pursue his passion or even to speak it out and express it to someone else. The belief system or the fabrication that the culture & society put on him became so strong that he never had faith in himself that he will ever amount to anything to anybody in life.

He often got scolded by his uncle for his inability to speak clearly & effectively and he was often a subject of criticism among his teachers for his lack of interest in academic or extracurricular activities.

One such day, when he finished his schooling time, one of the boys named Amrit came next to him and asked, "Hey Karamjit, are you even present here?"

"What do you mean? " replied Karamjit. "I mean, where are you lost all the time? You are lost in your own world"

Karamjit thought for a while, then buried his head in his arms as he folded them and sat down on the bench. "What happened? You Okay?" asked Amrit.

No answer came back. Not even a flinch. Amrit yelled back, "What's wrong with you? Do you think that someone cares to talk with you? You are such an egomaniac and an absolute narcissist which is the reason everybody avoids you because you don't know how to talk to people and make friends. " Karamjit winced at once and looked at Amrit with his calm poise. "It's not because of that." "Then What is it? Tell me!" "It's because people never really understand me." "And that's probably because you never tried to talk to them. You are into yourself. Isn't it?" Amrit asked. "Absolutely not. I was very open when I was a little kid but whenever I tried to express myself, people never took me seriously, ignored me and bullied me. Now how can a child who's been never given importance and always bullied come out to be socially constructive and interact freely with people? Maybe it's easy for others but surely it's not my cup of tea." "Why do you feel that? That's other people's business if they think you are not worthy of being listened to. At least I don't believe what they say about you." he assured .

"Really? You think so? But that's what I am told. I am treated as if I am a no good nick." "There is always a person in your life who always wishes for your wellbeing. So, you are telling me that nobody cares for you? Is that true?"

"No, I am not saying that. But most people I have met so far in my life showed me exactly that with their behavior towards me. The only person who is left in my life who really cares for me is my father. He is the only person who makes me feel good about myself and my uniqueness. He always says that I have some hidden abilities which I could manifest to help others. He is my best friend. But seldom do I get the opportunity to spend time with him" he said.

"Well, I believe in you. Trust me, I trust in you, and I have never felt that you are different than others even though they keep addressing you in a demeaning way. I never knew that you were such kind of a humble person. I always thought that you are an arrogant person who is too proud to mingle with others. That is why I never really talked to you before." said Amrit. "It seems to me that your father is your hero to you. Tell me something more about him."

Karamjit looked at Amrit and smiled as if he finally found the person, he was looking for all these years who would understand him. "My father is a Colonel and he's been serving in the Indian Army for the past 25 years. He is usually deployed at various different posts all throughout the year and help train young cadets to become future officers. And being an officer at a high rank like Colonel, he is also a consultant to the junior officers who train under his supervision. He has been deployed several times at some of the most difficult terrains whether it be in hot deserts or frost bite mountains. Besides that, he is a former national athlete who represented India at the 1990 Asian Games that were held in China." said Karamjit proudly feeling contented with his father's accomplishments.

"Wow! That's really awesome! He's one of an adventurous kind. I am really impressed by what your father has accomplished leaving me no doubt why he's your biggest inspiration." said Amrit. "Do you also have any plans to join Army?"

"No. I would never do that." said Karamjit as he turned his head around.

"But didn't you just said that you wish to be like your father?" "Yeah, definitely. He is my idol and I pursue to personify him in whatever I do, but my intention is not to go in the army but I want to live life on my own terms. I don't want to be someone who is under the supervision of an authority all the time which commands and dictates my life and how I should live or behave. I do desire to live an adventurous life. I want to travel around the world and meet with people who have similar interests. But...." Karamjit stopped as if something suddenly hit him.

"But what" asked Amrit. "No... nothing" replied Karamjit as if he were hiding something. "Are you sure?" "Yeah.... Nothing" he assured Amrit.

Amrit pat him on the back and gazed in his eyes. "Listen, I am just like your brother, so feel free to talk to me and open up your heart to me. Remember that I am always here to help you. And don't ever hesitate to share your mind with me. I am not like others. I want you to get this through your head. So always be open to me buddy. Do you understand that?"

"Yeah, I will keep it in mind. Thanks for your support." Karamjit shook his hand as he stood up. "Okay, I have to leave now." he said as he picked up his bag. "Do you have to go somewhere?" Amrit asked. "I have to go to Dukhniwaran Sahib Gurudwara for worship. I usually go there in the evening. Do you want to come with me?" "It's near to the place where I live. But I don't normally go to any religious places." "Why is that?" asked Karamjit.

Amrit looked up."Because I am an atheist. Although my parents believe in Hindu religion but I don't believe in the existence of God."

"Well, you can still come with me if you want. You just said that you are my friend, so must come with me." "Alright. I will meet you at the Gurudwara then. When will you reach there?"

Karamjit glanced at his Hungerford watch."Sharp at 6'o clock" he said. "Okay then, I will see you there." "Okay, bye buddy." said Karamjit as he bid him farewell.

Karamjit then hurriedly ran to his house with excitement of establishing a good friend in the image of Amrit in whom he can trust and share his thoughts. He was happy because he finally got someone who could listen to his story. His joy was out of bounds. He quickly reached home, had his lunch, and eagerly waited for the evening to occur.

Karamjit being a Sikh boy had his evening time scheduled to visit the Dukhniwaran Sahib Gurudwara for at least four days every week where he would spend his time listening to Gurbani. He would park his bicycle, remove his shoes, and deposit them to the Joda Ghar where all the visitors would deposit their shoes and slippers, then receive the token number specified for every visitor uniquely. He would then wash his feet and hands and walk forward to the Darbar Sahib – the main hall in the Gurudwara where Guru Granth Sahib is kept where he would chant his prayers and bow down to worship. He would keep sitting in the Darbar Sahib and listen with all his attention to the every word read from Guru Granth Sahib which is the holy scripture of Sikhism.

After that he would take a bath in the Sarovar—a rectangular open pool filled with sacred water with steps descending into the water. He would then take a walk on the sidewalks of the Sarovar with his hands folded all the while chanting his prayers. Amrit was with him that day. He was carefully observing Karamjit and all that he did in the Gurudwara as he visited with him the very first time. Amrit was amused by the lustrous look of the Gurudwara and its humungous size. He was very much impressed with the architecture of the Gurudwara and how the main building was paved. After walking around the Sarovar, they went to the Nishan Sahib. Amrit was shocked to see Nishan Sahib—a triangular flag hoisted on the top of a tall pole because of the height at which it was raised.

He taped Karamjit on the back as he lifted his head to look at the end point of the Nishan Sahib. " Why is that flag hoisted so high?" " It acts as a sign for the visitors so that it could be seen from far away, signifying the presence of Gurudwara in neighborhood. There is also a historical and spiritual significance to that." "What is that?" Amrit asked.

" It also serves as a sign of truth which leads people closer to the Eternal Guru or God in which Justice, truth and love reigns above all the hate, prejudice, and malice that prevails in this defective world or the Earthly realm. When you live righteously, it acts as a gateway to heaven." "Do you really believe in heaven?" "Yes, I do" Karamjit stated boldly. "It's a gift for your noble deeds from the God" he said.

"But I think heaven is merely a fictional concept which is good only for movies & children's novels. It's just an unrealistic place which people have created to escape the harsh reality of this world. And moreover, if it were real, why can't we observe it? I am very skeptical about all this spiritual realm jargon that people talk about. It's quite esoteric at least for me." Amrit said as folded his arms.

Karamjit looking at him and then giggled a little. " That's fine. That's your belief. And I respect that. But for me, heaven is more real than earth. You might not be able to perceive it, but it exist just like the air you breathe – you never see it but it still exists and gives you life." Karamjit pointed out. He took a deep breath and continued. "The same is also true when you walk on the righteous path and always do good to those who despitefully use you and even deceive you. Because God is always faithful with his promises and those who seek him with all their heart shall never perish."

Amrit was constantly staring at Karamjit with a look of skepticism as if he were looking for an opportunity to throw another ball of questions when Karamjit finished speaking. For Amrit, being an atheist, it was hard for him to conceive and believe what Karamjit was saying. "Really? Who defines this so-called righteous path? I mean, there is nothing absolute in this universe. What is right for me may not be right for someone else and what's right for them might not work for me at all. So this world is a whole conundrum between truth and false? Is that what you are saying?"

"Ha-ha-ha. I see that you have grasped Einstein's theory of relativity to a fair degree." said Karamjit in a witty manner as they both laughed out. "But there is always a creator or the ruler which sets the standard. He is the one who defines what is right and what is wrong. He is the one who separates light from darkness. He is the one who separates Truth from Ignorance. He is the one who sets dreams in the hearts of men and gives them the ability to fulfill them. He is the ultimate one who stands for the people who are righteous with his word" Karamjit said.

As soon as he said it, Amrit looked very anxious and confused. " I have had enough."he said. "Will you please explain to me what is this righteousness? How do you define it? I am not asking you to describe God or whatever you call him. I want you to tell me how do you decide whether someone is righteous or not?"

" Well, its no rocket science. Its quite easy actually. Righteousness simply means right alignment or positioning with God's standards. You do not necessarily have to wear religious clothes to be righteous. All you need to do is to not just seek your own individual good but the welfare of others and the whole community. Righteousness means to help others when they need you and doing works which help in uplifting others from low status to a rather high profile where they could do the same to other people they meet." he explained.

"Oh, I see. I believe that you are somehow different from all the religious people out there. I mean, the things that you say make some sense unlike the heavy words that those religious people throw at you just to puzzle you up. But it's not that easy Karamjit. There's a whole lot of difference between saying these things and then actually executing them in the practical life." Amrit remarked.

" There certainly is a lot of difference and that is the reason only few of the many are righteous because they have gone through the pain, suffering and hardships that walking on that righteous path requires. So it is difficult as you rightly pointed out. If it were easy, every other person would be righteous which is not the scenario, not in the contemporary world at least. You have to believe in the God when you have lost everything and even then continue doing the good works, only then can you attain that righteousness. And if you look at the history, you would find that there were very few people who were actually righteous and who endured that pain and suffering to attain and maintain it." Said Karamjit.

" Well.... Maybe you know quite a lot more than me in this context. But I am always skeptical about this concept as I have been in the past from a long, long time. I am understanding all you are saying and it even makes sense at the surface level but the real issues arise when you look at the problems with this theory at the micro level. What I mean to say is that I have seen and read about many people who struggled all their life and they never really got rewarded or appreciated by the society or even their own community for what they did. On the contrary, they were criticized by their own people. So, my question is: if they were walking on this righteous path that you were mentioning while facing all the hardships and turbulent times, then why is it that their efforts weren't recognized?" asked Amrit scratching his forehead.

" See, it's not about whether people appreciate or even recognize what good you have done for the others. They are not the ultimate judge even though they may make laws and legitimize them. Because even though, the society has its own measure by which it measures your actions, there still is the ultimate one who is above all the nations and national laws. He is the ultimate one who has created the universe and everything that exists in it. He is the ultimate judge. So he is the one who sees whether what you have done is righteous or unrighteous. It doesn't matter what people reward you for your efforts, but in the end what really matters is the appreciation that you get from the lord. Because he sees when no one is watching you. He knows everything. So if you are living a righteous life and even though nobody knows about it, he still knows it and appreciates you for doing that. That's what I meant" he explained.

" Oh, I see.... So you mean that there is a judgment for everything or every act that an individual commits in even the shortest moments of their life? Well, if that's the scenario, then its horrible for many people. Because the stuff that people do in their secret life, they don't want nobody to know about it." Amrit pointed out.

" Now you are getting it. So the crux of the matter is; if you are living a righteous life even when no one is watching you, then you are aligning yourself with that righteous path. Because remember, he always has an eye on you even when you think you are doing something secretly." Said Karamjit.

" Gotcha. Okay, I think we have had a good discussion on God. Now, my God is making some noises and he needs some food. So let's go and eat something." Said Amrit wittingly moving his hand on his belly.

" Ha-Ha-Ha. That's funny. We can go to the Langar hall. You will get some delicious food out there which would help you to relax your tummy." He said jokingly.

They continued straight to the Langar hall, a large hall where worshipers receive free meal while in the Gurudwara. Karamjit did his services in the Langar by serving food to the worshipers as all of them sat down on a long mat signifying equality for people of all castes, religions, and ethnicities. Amrit joined Karamjit in serving meal to visitors. After sometime, they too sat down to eat their meal which was served meticulously with chapatti, Dal and spinach with some salad.

Before eating his meal, Karamjit would fold his hands and pray to the Almighty.

Amrit could hear whispers from Karamjit while he was praying. He copied Karamjit and he too started praying joining his hands with a piece of cloth wrapped up around his head all this while. After finishing the meal, Karamjit went to the Joda Ghar to finish his part on storing other visitors shoes, slippers and then polishing them. It was a part of the services performed at the Gurudwara by the willing people. Amrit was along with him as he watched Karamjit quietly whispered into Amrit's ears. "Are you getting late? You can leave if you want to." "Are you not coming? How much more time will you stay here?" Amrit asked. "It won't take me more than ten minutes. I am almost done. You can stay if you want and then we can leave after some time." "Although, I had to study but alright, let's leave together then." Amrit responded as he glanced over Karamjit's Hungerford watch at once which struck 8'o clock.

They stood up as Karamjit removed a small rectangular piece of cloth that he tied around his waist so that the leather polish cannot stick to his clothes & make them dirty. They went over to the wash basin, washed their hands & feet, and left the Gurudwara building to catch up their vehicles to leave for their respective homes.

Karamjit went out and sat on his bike. "It was a good time together" he said. Amrit tapped him on the back as he jumped on to his bicycle. "I still have some questions which I want to ask you. I won't leave you until you answer all of them and leave me contented." Amrit said teasefully. "Ha-Ha. Sure, now that we are friends, we will have plenty time together discussing some interesting things." Karamjit replied. "Okay, then. See you tomorrow. Good night!" Karamjit lifted up his hand & waved as he bid him farewell. "Alright, Bye"

But Karamjit's day was never over until some trouble hit him giving him plethora of reasons for complaint. As soon as he reached home and opened the front door, he saw his aunt sitting on the sofa in the corner of the room, watching television while eating her chocolate chip cookies. He tried to rush quietly to his room without his aunt noticing him but failed. A loud voice struck his ears.

" You idiot! Where have you been all this time. Why have you reached home so late? I thought you only go to the Gurudwara but it seems you have slowly picked up your pace like the other squirrely teens looking for mingling parties. So you have also grown up your wings to fly huh? Do you think you have outgrown us you little dirty boy? Look at you, your clothes are all messed up. Oh.... You are such a disgrace to us. Speak up you dirty scoundrel!"

" Aunty, actually my friend....." " Friend what? Now, listen to me carefully. This is the last time I am cautioning you. If I ever come to know again that you are not at home by the evening time, you will face such a harsh punishment that you will not ever be able to think being persuaded to do this again. I might even send you to boarding school. Do you hear that?" Karamjit's jaw suddenly dropped and his tone became depressing. "Boarding school? No-No-No. Okay, I will never do that again. But please don't' send me to boarding school. Please, please...." "Now, shut your mouth, go eat dinner and then quietly sit down on your study table and start studying. Remember, I shouldn't have to remind you that again." Karamjit's aunt threatened him as he rushed immediately to his room and started studying.

While studying, his mind was wondering about Amrit. He thought about the meeting that he had with Amrit feeling a mixture of absurdity & excitement at the same time. Absurd because he never thought that he would be able to make a good friend which was an interpretation from the experiences that he acquired all throughout his life.

And excitement as he was ready to meet his friend again and speak up his mind to him which he couldn't do with any other person. It was due to this excitement that he wasn't able to sleep adequately that night. Due to lack of sleep, he woke up the next morning feeling low with an unusual pain in his back which was partially because he slept crumbled the whole night.

He rushed to school on his bike. This day was however different for him unlike other days. He was excited beyond measure and this was probably the first day in his life when he was excited & amused while going to school, singing on his way and one of the happiest moments of his life.

When he reached school, he quickly rushed pass the front door and entered the class with an unusual confidence that none of his classmates would ever witness from him on an average day. Karamjit would normally walk with his head down and dropped shoulders while his hands would be searching some lost treasure in his pockets. But today, he held his head high and chest out all the way swinging his arms in a harmonious way as he walked among the others. And everybody was a bit surprised at his unusual confidence that Karamjit was carrying along him.

But Karamjit being himself did not bothered about the staring eyes of his classmates and scanned the class looking for Amrit. He looked around the whole class but Amrit was nowhere. While he was thinking about Amrit's absence, a gentle tap came on his shoulders from behind and as soon as he turned around, he saw a beautiful girl who was one of his classmates standing next to him. "Are you looking for Amrit?" she asked him. "Yes, How do you know that?" "He told me to tell you that he is sitting right there in the canteen waiting for you." "Oh, I see.... Thanks for informing me." Karamjit said.

The girl quickly walked away without any response straight to a group of girls which to him appeared to be her friends. And all this while,

Karamjit stood there awestruck, looking at the girl until she appeared out of sight and suddenly Amrit came and shook Karamjit at once to wake him up.

He said, " Hey, didn't that girl inform you that I was in the canteen?" Karamjit nodded his head. "Yes, she did." " Okay, let's go to attend the class then. The lecture is about to start and you know that if you enter late then that rude, agnostic professor will throw us out of the class for the rest of the semester. Amrit warned him.

They both walked away for the class as Karamjit was still lost in his thoughts of that girl he just had encountered. " By the way, who was that girl? Do you know her? " Karamjit asked. Amrit started pacing up. " Oh, Yeah. She is my friend Riya. We are friends since our childhood. She lives in our neighborhood. " " Great!" Karamjit said.

2.

Trapped in the Snare

Many days passed and life went for Karamjit. One night, he was sitting on his study table with his room locked, rolling his pen between his fingers trying to focus on his homework grinding hard to understand the Calculus problems when suddenly his phone rang. He picked it up hurriedly and saw it was Amrit.

He was a bit surprised and skeptical thinking why had Amrit called him at such an odd hour of night? Is everything fine with him ? Could it be that something bad might have happened to him that he is calling me late in the night? He thought for a second. He went through all these thoughts in a matter of seconds and then picked up the phone.

" Hello..." he paused for a second and then continued "Amrit, is everything okay?" he asked with a clear intent in his mind. "Do you know the park that I visit every morning to exercise?" "Yes, the one on the Bhadson Road. Right? What happened?" he asked as he suddenly got up from his chair.

" This morning when I had just finished my running, I stopped nearby some benches to sit, take some rest and recover myself to prepare for some stretching as usual. And like every day, after gathering myself together, I set the timer for two minutes for stretching and kept it on one of the benches. As I got up, I saw an old guy probably in his 80's walking past me. When he went past me after some steps, his knees started trembling and he began to shake all of a sudden. I looked & thought that it could be a serious concern so I immediately ran towards him to give him a helping hand. As he was about to collapse, I took hold off him and called one other guy who was standing nearby. Two of us held him keeping his arms over our neck & shoulders and somehow we gathered him to put him on the bench. I instantly took my water bottle and asked him to drink some water to get him hydrated. He refrained from drinking water. He shook his head and said that he was fine. After about ten minutes, when he looked a bit relaxed, I asked him if he needs some help, he told me that he often encounter such short term paralysis in his lower body. He said that he was healed from paralysis a decade ago but still there is some effect that prevails. I asked to help him to take him to his home but he ignored my concern and said that he will call his son and return home and that I need not to worry about him. I asked him again but he reassured me with his gentle voice that he is doing well now." Amrit said all this in a single breath and took a pause to breathe and continue.

" What happened then? Did that old guy went home with his son?" Karamjit asked intrigued to know the complete story. "Yes, he sure was taken home safely by his family but when I got back to the spot where I was stretching, I was dumbstruck as I found my phone nowhere. I searched around every bench and every corner but I found it nowhere. I haven't told my parents about the incident yet. I don't know what I should do now. How careless I am! How can I tell them that I lost the phone due to my careless attitude? " Amrit said in a feeble voice.

" Umm... so you are telling me that somebody stole it. Right? Are you sure that you haven't forgot it placing somewhere else? " Karamjit asked. "I know it, for sure. I haven't misplaced it. Somebody has stolen it surely. I am definitely convicted about that" Amrit responded anxiously. "Alright, first of all calm down. Worry can't change nothing. We will sort it out. Should we report the matter to the police then?" "No-N0-No! No police! If my parents get to know about that, it would be terrible for me. We have to do something by ourselves. And don't tell anyone about this matter to anyone. Promise me that."

" Don't worry about your parents. We can convince them that it was none of your fault after all, you just tried to help that old man while someone took hold of the opportunity to steal your phone. They would definitely believe you and we can even figure out a solution readily after that. Their support would make the job easier. " Karamjit assured Amrit.

" No-No. See, you don't understand this. It's not that I don't want to be criticized for my carelessness by my parents. But I don't want them to put unnecessary stress on them because of my irresponsibility. I am grown up now and I must take complete responsibility of my life and possessions alike. So, please I urge you again don't tell the matter to anyone. I am affirming this to you iteratively that no one other than you and me should come to know about it. Do you get it? "

Karamjit started speaking in a low voice making sure his uncle and aunt can't hear him. He whispered in a low voice to Amrit. "Alright, but how are we going to do that? How in the world could we find who stole your phone?" he asked. "Well, I have an idea." "What is it?" "We can make use of the tracking application that can help us track my phone number and get to the thief's location to catch him red handedly." "Okay... but will it work?" Karamjit asked. "It sure will. Can you help me out with it?"

"I'll be glad to help you. Tell me what you want me to do?" "I'll meet you tomorrow morning outside the Environment park on Bhadson Road. Since school is off tomorrow, so meet me there at 9:00 a.m. and I'll tell you the plan. I need some time to think about it." "Alright" said Karamjit. "And don't worry thinking about it again. We will find the thief and get it done. Take some rest now and I will see you tomorrow." "Okay, Good night" Amrit said as he hung up the phone.

Karamjit too went to sleep early so he could get up early. The next morning, he got up only to realize that he was already late. He went to take the shower straight away and didn't ate his breakfast. He ran hurriedly to the park and saw Amrit with a worried look.

He went straight to him and tapped him on the back. "Hey, I am ready. So, tell me what we need to do?" "Give me your phone" Amrit took Karamjit's phone and pointed to the tracking app. "Look, this is the tracking application that I was talking about. If I can put my phone number and some details into it, it would probably give us the location of my phone making use of its I.P. address." "What are we waiting for? Let's go for it then!" Karamjit said immediately.

"Let's see, I will have to first put my IMEI number into it" "What is an IMEI number? Is it your mobile number?" he asked. "No, it's different than a mobile number. IMEI means International Mobile Equipment Identity. It's a unique number which is given to each user for their device which can help them to track their mobile's location." Karamjit began scratching his head. "Oh, I see. So, do you remember your IMEI number?" "I have already noted it before hand. And gosh, it saved me from a lot of trouble further!"

Amrit put the IMEI number of his lost phone with some details and tapped on the green button that read "Track". After about five minutes, a small window appeared on the screen with a list of three places where the probability of finding his phone would be maximum. It showed the location and the close proximity of his phone. "See, there it is. Its displaying the location of your phone!" Karamjit exclaimed. "But It's not precise at all. Its showing three locations, so we will have to go to all these places to search for it." Amrit argued.

The first place that showed close proximity of phone was near the Bhakra Nangal Dam on the Patiala Samana Road, the second one in Shakuntala Vihar near Tripuri market and the last one found in the Jhill Village leading to the Sirhind Road. Amrit put these locations on Google Maps and took hold of Karamjit's bike.

"Let's go and search for phone at each of these locations." he said. "Hand over the phone to me and I will tell you the directions" Karamjit sat on the back seat and they immediately rushed out of the place. Amrit followed directions as Karamjit guided him. They embarked to go to the Bhakra Dam first. After driving for ten minutes, they reached there and glanced at the location again on the phone. "Are we at the right place?" Amrit asked stepping off the bike. "At least, it says so. It is nearby, somewhere around there."

Karamjit said as he pointed out his finger to a small brick house which was right across the Dam. "Come, let's check it out" Amrit said. Both of them started marching straight to the house. As they reached closer and closer to that house, they realized that no one lived there. It had no door, no furniture and it appeared as if someone just piled up the bricks together haphazardly. The house was not cemented and there were cracks all over the place. Both of them went in, looked around hoping they would find the phone but their search did not last long as the wrecked up house had nothing more than some old rugged up bed sheets lurking on the ground. And some stale bread half eaten up by some animals probably a dog.

" There's nothing here " said Karamjit. "Not even another place in this locality where we can look out. No other house except this one where there is a possibility to find it" "Then we are left with other two places to go. It might be either of the other two" said Amrit. They quickly took their bike and went to the Shakuntala Vihar as per the guidance laid down by the map. As they reached there, they found the place to be a construction site. They tried to go ahead but were not allowed to pass through by the construction workers. So now, they were left with only one choice and that was to go and search out in the alleys of the Jhill village.

So they set out without squandering any time further and by the time they reached there, it was already noon. The streets in the village were narrow and there were very few natives of the town who lived there. Rummaging in the alleys of the village for about ten minutes, they finally reached the spot which the tracker identified. There was a house on the spot the tracker showed. The house was a rather small one with a narrow opening door. They stepped to the door and knocked over it twice. But no one came out. They knocked the door again but no one came out. Then they called out at the top of their voice asking if someone was there but all in vain as no one came out again.

Amrit left Karamjit's presence telling him that he would ask something from the neighbors. He told him to stay right there until he comes back to him. But even the closest houses in the neighborhood were all locked up. It seemed to him as if the whole place was completely deserted. Amrit went on and knocked on every door in the neighborhood hoping somebody might be living there and give them some insights about that particular house. Meanwhile, Karamjit kept standing right there in front of the door which they suspected to be thief's residence. He was waiting for Amrit to return but slowly he was losing his patience. So he knocked at the door once and as before, nobody came out. This made him mad and he pounded at the door with a hard fist.

Suddenly he lost his patience and put his left leg in between the space of the door steps and instantly jumped over the door thinking he would catch the thief and bring him to Amrit. He landed after jumping over the main door and as he walked in, he noticed that the interior door was unlocked, so he slowly and quietly stepped towards the room. But as he was about to enter the room, somebody shouted behind him saying, "Thief! Thief!" Karamjit trembled up in fear as a crowd gathered in the locality in just few seconds after the first cry. He heard someone saying, "Grab that bastard by his throat" and others saying, "Don't let him go. How dare he enter a house in that manner?" While some said,

"Look, how audacious he is! He thought he could get away with robbery in this daylight?" Before Karamjit could utter something, everybody around him had formed some preconceived notions about him and suddenly two sturdy tall men came jumping the door and grabbed him by his shirt collar. One of them slapped him on the back of his neck without letting him defend it. The other one pushed him forcefully, threw him out of the house and suddenly the crowd of the locality gathered around him as if they were thirsty for Karamjit's blood. Karamjit couldn't' speak anything as he was completely shivering when he saw too many people all surrounding him looking to almost kill him.

He somehow collected some courage and tried to speak but before he could utter a word, they started accusing him of an attempt of robbery. Someone in the crowd said, "Call the police, Now!" As Amrit returned, he saw the crowd and as he went ahead struggling to get past through the crowd, he saw Karamjit dusting off the ground. "What happened?" he asked Karamjit. "He stepped in that house and tried to rob it" a middle aged man answered as he moved his hand over his rounded belly which was about to un-tuck his shirts buttons.

" No-No-No! You are getting it wrong. He is not the thief. Instead, he came with me to help me catch the thief. Leave him alone please, he is innocent." Amrit said. "What are you talking about? I saw him myself stepping over that house door" said the middle aged man. "Let me explain it to you. Yesterday someone stole my phone and with the help of tracker we found out this house is where the thief lives. We knocked over the door many times but no one came out..." "So?" interrupted the man.

"Does that give him the right to jump over the door to enter someone's house like that without letting them know about it? I mean, how can someone do that, and that too in the daylight with every else present in the neighborhood? Now, the police will look into this matter. You can give all your explanation to them" he said. "But... please understand..." "No ifs and but's. I already told you that it's up to police now to look into this case." Amrit insisted to explain himself but all in vain. Soon, police came in a Jeep with a buzzing siren on top of it. And as they entered the locality, Karamjit almost fainted. He was terrified with thoughts of going to jail which would ruin his whole reputation. He thought at once of his uncle and aunt & felt guilty of giving this trouble to them.

Two Havildars stepped out of the jeep. They had their lathi's in their hands as they walked with their leather shoes making a thumping sound as they walked. They went to the people in crowd, talked to them and marched towards Karamjit. As they walked towards him, his heart started pounding. One of them grabbed him from his collar and tears rolled down his eyes almost immediately. They took him in the jeep and went away as Amrit stood there completely shocked and helpless to figure out what just happened. While everyone else around him went to their houses. He thought to himself: What would I say to his uncle now? All of this happened because of me. He just tried to help me and got himself into trouble. What should I do now? I think I should first go home and tell father and mother, the complete story of what happened.

He sat on his bike and went straight to his home. He hesitated at first but then revealed to his parents the complete story of how he lost his phone, then took help of Karamjit in finding it out which eventually placed Karamjit in the midst of difficulty.

Now, he was waiting to receive bashing from them. But contrary to what he was expecting, they told him to not to worry and said they'll somehow figure out the solution to this problem. Amrit was taken aback surprised by this response from his parents. He learned if he could have told about the issue to his parents earlier on, then all this would not have happened. His parents told him to first inform

Karamjit's uncle Gurtej Singh about Karamjit as he is a retired Armed Force personnel. So a person of his rank may have a significant influence and would get Karamjit easily out from the prison .

He went out and told Karamjit's uncle all about the incident. It was already evening by this time. Karamjit's uncle Gurtej Singh and aunt Jaswinder Kaur were all along there when he arrived at their home. He told them the whole story. After he finished, Jaswinder kaur burst out angrily looking at Gurtej Singh. "See, I told you that we shouldn't give that boy this much freedom to go outside of home. Look what he has done. He is a complete disgrace to us and our reputation. We cannot take responsibility for his actions anymore. Let him do what he wants to do and let's just separate ways from him. "Calm down darling, Calm down please." "What do you mean calm down? He is completely ruining our name in the society."

" Don't you know that Karamjit isn't that kind of a boy. He can't even imagine of robbing someone in his wildest dreams. Haven't you listened to what Amrit has said? And after all, you have been with Karamjit for almost a decade now and you still haven't figured him out? Anyhow, don't worry. We are going to sort out this matter together. " said Gurtej Singh as he immediately went taking Amrit with him in his Ambassador to the Police Station where they might have kept Karamjit.

As they entered the police station, they saw some prisoner's locked up while some others were sitting on the bench adjacent to the locker room. Gurtej Singh saw Karamjit sitting among them with his head buried in his arms. "Karamjit!" he shouted .Karamjit lifted his head up as he heard a voice he recognized very well. "Uncle!" he shouted. "Please take me out of here. I have stolen nothing. Believe me" " I know Dear. You cannot do this. Don't worry, I will take you out of here." The prisoner's in the cell were making some strange noises which even further terrified Karamjit as he got piled up in the corner of the bench that he was sitting on. His heart was getting pounded every time the prisoners started shouting at each other. He was imagining himself sitting in the cell with the same prisoner's that were shouting and behaving like complete psychopaths.

Gurtej Singh asked the Inspector who was sitting on his desk with his feet on it while his head was dug in his phone. "Inspector" he said. "On what evidence have you put my nephew here in the prison? Did he stole anything? Do you have any evidence which proves him guilty?" he asked.

The Inspector gazed at him once lifting up his hat with his fore finger and then continued to scroll through his phone as if he didn't noticed him. "I am speaking to you, Sir. Do you hear me? Please show me the evidence." He repeated. The Inspector turned down his phone on the desk and dragged his chair forward and said, "Sit down Please" "No thanks. Will you please respond to my queries?" "Listen Sardar ji, we have prospects who have given statements against that boy saying that he entered the house to attempt robbery. In fact, there are not just one or two, but many who saw and caught him red-handedly trying to sneak into one of the rooms of that house." he explained. "But did you found something that he stole? No, you didn't. Right? So you can't just take him under your custody based on what you have heard others say." "Yes I understand law better than you I suppose. And believe me, our team is going to introspect into this matter deeply. Rest assured, if he is innocent then he will be set free out of the prison soon." "Listen Inspector, I am a retired Army personnel with many rewards and heroic achievements under my belt. And that boy has grown up under my supervision and guidance, so I know he can't even think of committing such acts. So you better do something fast and sort it out quickly." He warned.

"Hey, Hey, Hey. It doesn't work that way with the police. Alright? You need to be polite and gentle if you want thing to get done here. This is not your army platoon where you are the leader and shout out your commands to your subordinates. This is a police station and if you want something to get done here then it goes through the required checks and balances. So, shouting and whining can do nothing except to delay the process." Said the inspector. "Whatever.... Just make sure that you release him as soon as possible." Gurtej Singh demanded.

"Take some rest Sardarji. I see you are breathing heavily. Its not good for you to take stress at this age. Please sit there on the chair" the inspector said in a mocking tone with no clear intention to take Gurtej Singh seriously.

Gurtej Singh looked apart absolutely appalled at the Inspector's narcissistic behavior and sat on the chair kept near the long bench on which Karamjit was crumbled up.

Meanwhile, Amrit went to see Karamjit. He placed his hands over his shoulders trying to relax him. "Karamjit, Don't worry. We are going to get you out of here" he said. "It's all my fault. I shouldn't have jumped over the door and should have waited for you instead. That would have saved me from troubling all of you." He murmured. "Don't be silly brother. You were just helping me. You don't have to feel the guilt at all. It's not your fault. We were already knocking at the door for quite a long time but no one came out." " But I have also put my uncle under distress. I am a complete disgrace for everyone else " "Don't say that brother. Just calm down " Amrit comforted him as he put his arm over his shoulder to rub off and make him feel accepted. He sat with him there and thought how he could solve this catastrophe. Then he somehow remembered Riya. " Hey, do you remember Riya?" he asked Karamjit. "Yeah, that beautiful girl who lives in your neighborhood. Right? " "Yeah, Do you remember I told you that her father is a commissioner in the Ludhiana district? Maybe she can help us out." " You think so? Try it out " "Yeah, definitely. Let me contact Riya and tell her the whole drama. She is my good friend. She can help us out." Said Amrit. And Karamjit simply looked in quiet desperation hoping to get out from there soon as he was getting nervous with every minute that passed by making him realize again that he made a huge mistake by doing such a small act which led him to such a problem.

Amrit dialed Riya's number using Karamjit's phone and waited for her to pick it up. The call just rang and rang and rang but no one picked up the call. He called again but ended up in the same result again. Meanwhile, Karamjit was getting nervous and his whole body was covered up in sweat because of the induced fear that crept upon him and he started shivering. Amrit tried calling Riya again after about five minutes and this time by the God's grace, she picked up the phone and before she could ask anything, Amrit gulped out the story. "Hello Riya, this is Amrit speaking. This is very urgent. I want to ask you for something...." And he went on to explain the whole story after which he asked if she could help them in any possible way. "Well, let me ask my father. He shifted to Ludhiana 3 years back but he still certainly has some connections in Patiala's police department.

"Great, please let me know if it can help. And by the way, you have already met Karamjit before. Right? You know he is a nice guy and he can't do this stuff." "What are you talking about Amrit? If you are asking for this, I don't even have to ask if he is innocent or not. I know you and you understand him. Right? Trust is the key. That's the biggest thing that glues us all together. Okay, just wait a second and I'll let you know what my father says once I talk to him on phone." "Thanks a lot Riya! You don't how much of a help you have been to me always. I really appreciate that." He said. "No worries, Amrit. We are friends and it's common in friendship to do these little things." "Okay, please do let me know then." "Sure" said Riya as she hang out the phone.

Amrit desperately started waiting for Riya's call to get some information from her father. Meanwhile, Gurtej Singh started calling his advocate friends from the military's JAG department to get some advice on the matter. But he got no real quick advice from them and all of them told him to wait for another one day as offices were closed that day. Amrit went to him and told him that he contacted Riya who could help them as her father is a commissioner. And Gurtej Singh just sat there with no response holding his walking stick looking absolutely annoyed at the inspector's behavior.

After about 10 minutes, Amrit picked up Riya's call and she said, "Amrit, my father has said that he wants to talk to the chief of that police department which you are in." "Yeah, sure. He is sitting right here. Let me hand it over to him." "Okay, let me put the call on conference and call my father." She said. Amrit went over to the inspector and handed over the phone to him. "Sir, this is the head commissioner of the police department of the Ludhiana district and he wants to have a discourse with you. So please….." "Hello?" said the inspector as he took hold of the phone. And Amrit kept standing there hearing attentively what the inspector was saying. Gurtej Singh also got up from his chair as the inspector went on to a deeper conversation with Riya's father.

The inspector hung up the phone and gave it to Amrit. "Here, take it away." He said. He called someone with his phone and said, "Let's go for a search in that home" and placed the phone back on desk. "Havildar, take that boy and let's go to the place where he told us about the suspect." Gurtej Singh hurried to inspector. "What happened? What did he said?" he asked. "Let's go to that location where we caught your nephew and if he is speaking the truth, his phone might be somewhere around there but if it's not found there, we can do nothing other than to punish him."

They went taking Karamjit with them in their Jeep with one Havildar sitting on the back seat with Karamjit. While, Gurtej Singh and Amrit reached there in his Ambassador car. After reaching the location for riding in the jeep for 10 miles, they stepped out of the car with Karamjit coming steadily along with the Havildar. They took him out of the jeep with his shirt collar in their hand. "So, where is that house?" asked the Inspector. "That one" Karamjit pointed out with his finger. "So, is this the one according to you where you were searching for the lost phone? Are you sure about it?" asked the Inspector. "Yeah, the detector showed that it was this house" he replied hesitatingly. "Let's go Damodar" he said to the Havildar.

They went on to the house and knocked on the door three times after which a voice came from inside the house. "Coming.... Please wait. Oh, it might be the delivery boy with my pizza." The man said. As soon as he opened the door and saw the police standing there, his face became pale and he asked, "Yes? May I help you please?" "What is your name?" the inspector asked. "B-B-Bhola" the man replied stutteringly. "We need to check your house" "But you can't do that" the man said firmly. "What? What did you just said? Why can't we, Huh?" the inspector asked agnostically. "I mean, do you have the right to do it? Show me your search warrant. How can I let you search my house without a written consent from the authorities?" "Here it is, See."

The inspector said as he pulled out a small letter unfolding it and handed it over to the man to read. "Seen? Now, get aside and let us do our work". The Inspector along with Havildar Damodar got through the main door into the lobby of the house and then entered the front room.

"Damodar, search in every corner of the room. Leave no piece of furniture unturned." he ordered Damodar. "Sir!" replied the havildar in a rather high spirit voice. They inverted the furniture, book shelf, searched the whole kitchen, tucked the bed sheets upside down, searched behind the closet but found the phone nowhere. "Let me give a call and maybe it will ring somewhere around here." Said Amrit suddenly.

"Yes, dial your number." Said the inspector. Amrit dialed his number from Karamjit's phone and all of a sudden they heard the bell ringing. "There it is, There it is. It's my phone's ringtone" said Amrit excitedly. "But where is the phone? It's ringing from that room" said the inspector as he pointed to the next room adjacent to the kitchen. They rushed into the room and Amrit dialed the number again and to their amazement, the phone was lying on the bottom of the shoe rack.

The inspector picked up the phone and showed it to Amrit. "Is it your phone?" "Yes, yes!" he exclaimed. "Damodar... grab that bhola and take him to the police station." he ordered. "Sir-Sir, please leave me please. I swear, I won't repeat this mistake again in my life ever. Please, Sir. I am a poor man so I have to steal to eat my bread. Have some mercy over me, please." Bhola pleaded. "You should have thought of the consequences before making this decision. Law is equal for every individual. Once you have committed a crime, however trivial or insignificant that maybe, you will get punished and face the repercussions for that. Damodar, take him with us. And all of you, please come with us so we can remove charges against this boy." Said the inspector.

They moved to the police station and finally Karamjit felt relieved as he saw the inspector removing charge of robbery against him. Amrit also learned a very important lesson with this incident which got ingrained in his mind that it's better to be responsible than to reap misery followed with ignorant decision making. Gurtej Singh was happy as he kissed Karamjit on his forehead. "I knew, you were innocent. Doing these things is below you." He said.

All of them went home and Gurtej Singh after reaching home, said to Karamjit to simply take some rest as he was already tired. Karamjit rarely saw this avatar of Gurtej Singh as normally he would be rude and foul-mouthed towards him. And Gurtej Singh was full of pride because he finally saw his younger self in Karamjit who tried to help his friend with all his strength and might.

3.
Hidden Desires Perpetuates

After some days, Karamjit went to school again. That day while he was rummaging through the corridor of the school building,, he saw Riya walking down the stairs. He went straight to her. "Hey Riya!" he said as he waved his hand up. She turned around looking at him after a second said, "Hey Karamjit. How you doing now?" "Umm... good. How are you?" "Terrific." She said. Karamjit stood there expecting her to initiate the conversation further. As she spoke nothing, finally he said, "Thanks a lot Riya for helping me out." "Thanks? For what?" "Don't you remember you helped to release me from the prison against the false allegations put on me?"

"Listen, we are friends. So it's normal in friendship to do these small acts and never even talk about it. Don't you know that?" she whispered. "Friends?" he asked taken aback by surprise. "Yeah. Okay, I have to go to attend my class now. We'll meet sometime again. And remember there are no 'apologies' or 'thanks giving' in friendship" she said as she hurried down the stairs and left out of his sight quietly.

Karamjit stood there looking her leave and completely surprised. He thought to himself: Did she really say friends? Woah.. a beautiful girl like her calling me her friend without me even talking to her for a significant period of time. This was something that he had never experienced before so He told about this to Amrit while they were leaving the classes with absolute amusement in his eyes like a little kid. "Why are you so excited man?" asked Amrit. "She called me her friend!" he exclaimed. "Oh, come one. She calls every other person her friend after she meets that person. She don't even give it a second thought while saying it." "Really?" he asked. "Yeah, don't ponder over it too much." Said Amrit. And in a moment, Karamjit lost all his excitement and slouched his shoulders. “By the way, are we going to Gurudwara this evening? Let’s go there huh? It’s been a while since we have been there.” asked Amrit.

“Hmmm... let’s go” Karamjit replied in a rather disappointed tone. “Also I forgot to convey to you that Riya was asking if you were fine after that incident. So, you might have told her today I suppose.” “Yeah, I talked to her but she had to attend her class so she left soon.”

In the evening, they went to the Gurudwara as usual but as Karamjit was serving the Langar to the worshippers, he saw Riya sitting in one of the lanes. As he went to her to deliver the bread, she looked at him and smiled at once. Karamjit felt mesmerized by her smile and he couldn’t help himself but smile too. After langar, he met with Riya as she was washing her feet in the Sarovar. “Hey” said Karamjit as he waved his hand to Riya. “Hello” she replied as both glared in each other’s eyes without saying a word. She felt embarrassed all of a sudden with that momentarily collision of their vision with each other and turned her face the other way.

“ So are you coming to school tomorrow?” he asked casually. “Why wouldn’t I? I never miss my classes unlike you” she said wittingly. Karamjit felt her humor as they both giggled a bit. They were feeling the cool breeze of the night sky in each other’s presence when all of a sudden Amrit shouted from a distance. “Hey Karamjit, come on let’s go home now. Otherwise, your aunt will not spare you again if you reach late. Come fast, I am waiting for you at the parking lot” he said. Karamjit looked at Riya and then glanced over his Hungerford watch realizing it was time for him to leave for home. “Okay then, we’ll meet tomorrow.” “Sure” she replied. “Good night and take care” he said as he left for home.

Karamjit went home and got lost in his thoughts as usual but this time it was Riya who tinkered his imagination. He met her the next day in school and spent some time with her in the spare time after the classes were over. It was everyday routine for them now to meet in the school and then in the Gurudwara in the evening time for their chit-chat. They would continue to talk for long hours, Riya being the more talkative one, was obsessed about telling her life to Karamjit. While Karamjit would quietly listen to her getting lost in her glaring eyes all this while. Amrit would see all of that. It was quite obvious for Amrit now that they both had a liking for each other. So he would also give them their space to spend time with each other and get to know about each other as well as they can.

Karamjit would usually ask Riya to miss some of their classes and instead go on a walk in a park nearby where they would sit all by themselves. She resisted at first but then she agreed with him and went with him to spend some time with him. She seemed to be a quiet and introverted girl at first but later on, as Karamjit spend more and more time with her, he found out that she is way more talkative than he could ever have thought. Riya would continue to tell her stories and Karamjit would just listen to her soothing voice with serenity of mind.

One fine day, they were sitting in a park and Riya asked Karamjit, "So, what have you thought of doing after passing out from the 12th standard?" "Uhh.... I don't know. I haven't thought of anything yet." "Are you kidding me? Haven't you thought what your goals or ambitions are?" she wondered. "Not really. What have you thought about? What are your plans?" he asked Riya knowing he would get a long reply of the tongue from her as he waited excitedly to listen.

"Well.... My aspiration is to become a pilot in the Indian Air Force. I always wanted to fly and measure the vast expanses of the sky. When I was younger, my father used to take me to visit the seashores and in the cool breeze, I used to wander looking at the seagulls and birds flying over the sea. I always used to wonder: what would it be to be like one of these birds to expand their wings and dive in the sky, being free from every stress or problems of the world. Just living with the flow of the air. So, I thought that one day, I would become an Air force pilot and take flights just like those birds. That is the true freedom for me. Freedom to fly, freedom to not worry about anything that could ever happen with my life, freedom to live on my own terms, freedom to do what I love to do, freedom to go where I want to go, freedom to be who I want to be, and freedom to choose my own destiny."

"Well, that's really great!" Karamjit replied as she stopped for a moment to inhale some air. "But you know what? There are some people in the world who believe that since I am a girl, a female, it's not civilized for me to hustle for my dreams. My dad always supports me but I have met some people who do not appreciate that girls should grind for what they aspire to do. But anyhow, I don't listen to any of those people. Because my father always taught me that I can always achieve whatever I can conceive and believe. Whenever I failed at any moment in my life, he never discouraged me to never try again. In fact, he told me to always learn lessons from my failures and then move ahead in life stronger than ever. Although I am still naïve, I do believe that that's the essence of life: to always keep learning."

"Wow... You know what? Whenever I listen to you, it reminds me of my mother. I was very young when I lost her but I still have some fond memories of her taking care of me and the lullabies that she used to recite to me. In a way, your thoughts are so insightful and you add much more meaning to the words you say. Your thoughts are so much coherent with the way the life works. Well, you can always try your hand on philosophy if you want." Karamjit said jokingly.

"Whaaaaaat?" she said as they both burst out laughing. "Did you just say philosophy? Well, that was a good one though" "No, but seriously. Your thoughts are deep just like a philosopher. If I ever would have a mentor, I would like that person to be a philosopher. The time that I have spent with you so far, I have come to know that you are a critical thinker. You don't just accept things as true even though it's pressed upon by some authority. You take the information that you heed, then you dissect it down and see its various fragments and then check whether it aligns with what the other person has said or not. I mean, that's a very good quality that you have which makes you smarter than almost everybody else I have met in my life" he said.

She started smiling when he made this statement. "Okay, so now you have started flirting huh? But you are not very good at that I see" she said. "No- no-no, I really mean that. You are a skeptic and I really appreciate that quality which is very rare in the people that I have met so far in my life at least. Maybe that sounds cheesy to you but I really do mean what I have complemented you on." He said.

"Okay, okay, okay. Don't be so serious. I was just kidding to see your reaction to it. I must say you don't get tempted easily either. So, that's a nice quality to have too." She said as Karamjit started blushing. "Now you are being too generous" "And you too cute" she replied. "And I would suggest you to think about the things that really interest you or you feel passionate about." She said. "Okay, I will do it." "By the way, I know that you like me. Right?" Karamjit was just shocked and couldn't believe what he heard from her. He wasn't able to speak and started gasping for breath to calm himself down. "What happened huh?" she said with a giggle. "Well, don't worry. I like you too. I mean, we are good friends . Don't we? And after all we have spent quite a lot of time together, so we understand each other better now. So, we'll meet tomorrow then. See you, bye" she left immediately as soon as she finished speaking.

While Karamjit stood there still trying to recover his senses back to normal trying to believe that what he heard was true. He was surprised, excited and shocked simultaneously as it was his first time in life that he ever heard a girl say that she likes him. He couldn't believe it. He called Amrit immediately and told him about it. And Amrit listened to him until he finished and then said, "So what? Why are you so surprised? You didn't knew about it? I mean, it was visible to me from the very beginning that she was interested in you." "What? Why didn't you tell me about it?" "Well, I thought you would be knowing it as you were spending so much time with her. You were spending almost two-third of your time with her. Matter of fact, I should be asking you this question of how could you be so ignorant about this thing? It's a surprise to me that you didn't knew about it." "Yeah, I also like her. So ,what should I make out of it? Is it love?"

"See Karamjit, it's difficult to say on that part. I don't think that you should really consider it love. It might be infatuation as well. You never know when it happens. It might be simply attraction as a friend. It might just be an authentic curiosity to know more about the other person. So, I can't really make anything out of it other than that you both like each other. That's the crux of the matter for me." "Do you think I should talk about it with her openly? I mean, to just discuss what's going on or will it be better to just let the things flow as they are for some time until the right time comes?" "I think you should discuss and share your mind with her. Spend some more time with her to sort the uncluttered things in a lucid way so that you don't face any repercussions of any sort in the future. So, don't take this thing too seriously also. I have seen many people who have ruined their lives just because they took their infatuation and called it love. And the ramifications that they had to deal with later on were intense and often brutal in some cases. So please make sure that you don't complicate things and keep them as simple and straight as possible. I would advice you to talk to her and don't create unrealistic expectations in your mind from any person whatsoever, otherwise you will face plenty trouble." "Alright, so

I will talk to her about this issue the next time I meet her. Goodbye and thanks."

Karamjit hung the call confused of what he should consider doing now. It was the very first time in Karamjit's life that somebody was getting so close to him and that he could relate to. It was not just emotional or psychological alignment which led him to like Riya. But it was also his natural, physical & sexual desires that were driving him crazy about her that he couldn't help himself but to think about her all day long. He was so much obsessed with her thoughts that he couldn't even focus on his studies. It was difficult for him to maintain his focus on one thing that could set apart her existence.

The only time which he felt pleasant was when he was with her, listening to her talk he would feel an absolute harmony in his spirit that he would be a different person altogether in her presence but back to the old Karamjit who was scared and skeptical in her absence. In a way, he became addicted to her being close to him that it would become unbearable for him to even imagine going through a day without meeting her. One day, he couldn't resist the temptation to talk about his situation and what he's going through after meeting with her.

So he gathered all of his courage and spoke in a firm voice. "Riya, I wanted to share something with you." She was rolling her hair in her fingers and casually said, " Yeah, tell me. What is it?" "Umm... Actually.... Uhh... actually I have felt a lack of focus in whatever I try do in these last couple of days. I am not able to perform even my regular tasks with the same efficiency. And it also prevents me from focusing on my studies." "What happened? Are you sick? Let me check your temperature." She asked worriedly as she placed the back of her hand on his forehead. "No... I am perfectly good. It's not sickness nor pain of body" "Then what is it? Feel free to tell me."

"Uhh... it's actually you. The things is, whenever I am sitting idle, I cannot stop myself from thinking about you. I cannot focus on other things because your thoughts keep striking my mind every time I try to do something. I don't know what is it. But that's what it is." "Oh-ho-ho. Now, don't tell me that I also have a visitation in your dreams" she laughed it out. "How do you know that? You do visit even in my dreams. It has become so intense for me. I just wanted to share it with you and keep no secret any longer." "It's good that you have shared it with me. But you know what, I also go through the exact same experiences that you mentioned. I think we know each other too well now and we have become more than just best friends. Don't you think so?" "I do believe so. It's a strange feeling for me as I have never been so close to a girl in my life as I have been to you." "Never mind. But I like you no matter what you think about it." "Well, I like you too. And finally I want you to know that." "Ha-ha, I knew it already from the very day you met me in the school. But for the time being, let's not go farther than just being best friends. I think that would be the best possible scenario for both of us to incorporate in our life" "I promise that" he replied feeling relieved that he opened up his feelings with her.

4.

Getting Derailed.....

Life went on for Karamjit as he continued his normal everyday living; going to school; waiting to meet Riya desperately and looking forward to spare some good time with her. Meanwhile, he was spending lesser and lesser time with his friend Amrit now who was almost separated from him due to scarcity of time and changing of priorities in his life. His relationship with Amrit was getting affected as he couldn't talk to him much now. But he wasn't aware of it as he found a best friend cum lover in Riya whom he used to listen to talk in her soothing voice. He could have done it all his life if he wanted to because he was never tired of hearing her speak. So life seemed to him without any worries at this stage.

But it's an irony of fate that whenever he thought that life went by seamlessly for him, it was at that moment that a catastrophe would hit him with a huge blow. One day, while he was sitting on his study table trying to concentrate on the Nuclear Physics, he heard the landline telephone ringing. It was unusual for him as it was rare that someone would call at home on the landline telephone. So he stood up from the chair and went into the lobby to pick up the phone. But before he could do that, his uncle Gurtej Singh arrived there and picked the phone up. "Hello" he answered. "Gurtej Singh speaking?" the voice in the telephone asked. "Yes, who is this?" Gurtej Singh asked. He stood there for a minute sticking the telephone close to his face. His face started to grow faint with every passing second. Suddenly, the telephone slipped past his weary hands and he sat down on the couch like a sack of potatoes mashed up. "What happened Uncle?" Karamjit shouted as he saw his uncle distressed. He shook his uncle's shoulders at once and asked him again if he was fine. "Are you okay, uncle? Whose call was it?" "It was from your father's battalion" he said in a rather feeble voice. "Oh Great , so is he returning back from his posting. Well, that's awesome. I can spend some time with him now. It's been almost a year since he has visited here." He looked at his uncle's face which was elongated in an unusual fashion. "Aren't you happy?" he asked. "Father is visiting us after a long, long time" "He is not visiting us." Gurtej Singh said. "Why?" "Because he is dead" he wept out loud.

Karamjit stood there shocked at what he just heard. He couldn't believe it. "You are just kidding. Right?" he asked. Gurtej Singh grabbed him in his shoulders and started weeping. "He is no more" he cried out. "They said he died in an operation where one of the enemies bullets hit him at his right shoulder and the other passed through his stomach leaving him wounded. They took him to the military hospital as soon as they can, got him treated but the wounds were so deep that he couldn't survive them." He blurted out crying. Karamjit started weeping too as he hugged his uncle tight.

Meanwhile, his aunt Jaswinder Kaur stood behind them watching them but did not even flinched. It didn't even mattered to her whether his father died or lived. She pretended to cry and moved her hand over Karamjit's face trying to be empathetic towards him. "How bad it is... Oh lord, how many troubles have you kept in account of this boy? Have some mercy on him." She cried out loud.

Life again took this sadistic turn for Karamjit. He, along with his uncle and aunt were invited to the military funeral of his father which took place in Khadakwasla, Pune. The crematorium was some few miles away from the National Defense Academy (NDA) of which Balkar Singh was a cadet and graduated in 1985. So they packed their luggage to visit the crematorium ceremony as it was the last opportunity for Karamjit to get a glimpse at his father.

There were plethora of military figures in the crematorium and the silence of the day was broken by the beating of the drums. And the funeral service began with the beating of drums followed by a 2 minute silence for the dead soldiers and officers among which Balkar Singh was one. Then followed blowing the bagpipers, the firing of volley shots as a salute and giving away the guards of honor to the martyred soldiers and officers for the dedication and the commitment that they displayed in keeping the country protected even though they had to pay the price with their own lives.

When the ceremony was finished, Karamjit went ahead to see the face of his father along with his uncle Gurtej Singh. His feet trembled as he was approaching the coffin with a bouquet of flowers. When he faced the glass coffin with his father's face and eyes closed in tranquility, tears rolled down his eyes almost immediately and he fell on his knees crying out loud. Gurtej Singh felt tempted to pick him up but resisted the urge to do so thinking to let Karamjit outflow his emotions for a while. Gurtej Singh then tried to comfort him with a pat on the back and pick him up. Karamjit did not resisted, he turned his face up and gave a salute to his father for his absolute determination and sheer persistence to face and relish in times of adversity. He started moving away from the coffin, never looking back again with tears still rummaging through his cheeks.

After the ceremony, Karamjit stood there standstill at the officer's mess while Gurtej Singh had some conversation with some of his old colleagues and batch mates from the Officers Training Academy (OTA) Chennai. Meanwhile, Karamjit stood behind him lost in his thoughts and memories of his father. Some officers comforted him with their words while others just stood there with him in complete silence marking respectful demeanor for the martyrdom of a legend and a warrior that his father was. Some shared with him the stories of how his father had amazing military skills and leadership qualities which separated him from his followers. And how he always reflected the best in his team mates so that they could unleash their true potential.

Some said his father was rude and sturdy sometimes, to some of the people citing the reason for this that it was to help others grow and become better than they were the day before. While others said he was kind and compassionate in his time off the duty and would treat everybody like his best friends. There were many storytellers at that day who were citing the stories of his father's bravery, courage, and determination to serve the country to the best of his ability. But Karamjit was lost in his mind with the words of his father still resonating in his mind iteratively.

When they came back to Patiala city, Karamjit couldn't move out for several days and he would just keep sitting in his room staring at the wall for hours lost in his father's memories. It was a big loss for him as there were only very few people in his life who actually understood him and his father was one of those very few. He would get calls from Amrit and Riya but he wouldn't answer them and just sit crumbled up in his room quietly.

He wouldn't eat most of the times due to which he was shrinking and losing weight. Gurtej Singh was worried as he saw Karamjit's condition which was getting worse day after day. He would urge him to eat something but all in vain. He was almost moving into a state of depression. And Gurtej Singh felt that it would be better for him if he could mingle with his friends and have some conversations which would allow him to throw off some of the burden from his shoulders that he is carrying for so many days of his father's death and the regret of not being able to meet him for the last time.

So he called Karamjit's friend Amrit to their home so that he could talk to him and make him feel better. Amrit came immediately as a good friend would normally do. "Hey Karamjit, what's up dude? How you doing? Long time, no see huh?" he said as he entered the room and jumped on his bed. But Karamjit kept sitting there rolled up and gave no reply. And Amrit could feel the pain Karamjit was going through just by looking at his face. "Hey, come on. Let's go take a walk outside. That would make you feel better. Come on, let's go" he said as he hold his arms and tried to get him off the bed. "No. I don't want to go anywhere. Leave me alone please" said Karamjit. "Listen man. I can understand the loss that you have encountered of your father who was your mentor, your friend, and the person you looked up to as an inspiration for yourself. But now just leave what's happened in the past and move into the future." "It's not so easy Amrit." He said. "I know it's not easy and I am not saying it's easy at all. But what I want you to understand is that you cannot change the things that happened in the past but you have the power to shape the future by choosing to plan what you do in the present. Don't leave any regrets piling up in your mind that will consume your conscience. Get out of your rut and move ahead. You know, the worst way to drive is to look into the rear view mirror and if you do that, there could be nothing worse than that."

" I understand that. But it's difficult to see the whole picture when you are trapped in the box. And looking at my condition right now, I can say that I am that person trapped in the box right now. So it's easy for you to look at things and formulate a good decision but not for me, not at least in this time."

" Okay, I won't persuade you to try and change your mind but let's just go on a walk for some time at least. I can ask at least this much as a friend. Can I ? " he asked. " Alright. Let's go on a walk in the park. Maybe, you are right, it will help me think in a clear and concise way." He said as both of them got off the bed and took their bikes to go to the park. They did some running and then some stretching workout leaving them covered in sweat after which they sat down on the bench quietly without any of them saying anything. They were just staring at the grass and the ants carrying the sugar on the dump of sands. And Amrit finally broke the silence. " Have you met with Riya recently?" "No, it's been a couple of weeks since I last met her after my father's demise." "She actually called me a lot of time asking about you and your well being." " I actually feel guilty as I was not answering her calls. She called me many times too just like you did. But because I was so depressed that I could not think clearly of what I should do" "Don't worry about that. She has a very understanding attitude and probably she knows it already by now that it's naturally for someone to behave that way when they loose some loved one. You can get it sorted out by meeting her. She would get it" " I will meet her tomorrow then."

Karamjit called Riya and asked her to meet him the next day as he didn't have any plans to go to school. And they met the other day sitting all by themselves quietly when Riya asked, "So, how are you doing now? Is it better than before?" "I feel quite well now. Yesterday I had some conversation with Amrit and it made me feel better. Actually I had to apologize to you for not picking up your calls. I don't want to make excuses but I was really depressed at that moment and couldn't think in the right way. I hope you will understand it" he said. "Oh- no! No need to apologize. You have lost your father and I know how much I love my father. And if somehow, I lose my father, I would probably lose my mind because he is my world to me. So I don't blame you for not picking up my calls. And moreover, we are back together again, so we will sort out the issues and you will soon get back to normal life. I promise you that. Just let me know whenever you need any help from me." "Thanks a lot Riya. You are a true example of a best friend" "Or am I more than just a friend" she said wittingly. And they both started smiling. It was the first time that he smiled after his father's death. As Karamjit started spending time again with Riya, he felt that he got out of this conundrum of depression finally.

He now continued his school and his studies normally meeting with Riya and Amrit who were still his only friends at that time. And in a time frame of few days, his life went back to normal. He got his time covered up in doing daily household chores as he also developed a keen interest in gardening which was a result of staying with Riya as she was also into gardening. She would give him the plants from the nursery and he would plant them in his own house garden.

Meanwhile, Gurtej Singh was happy now as he saw Karamjit getting back to normalcy. But his aunt as always had no interest in seeking his happiness and would always seek ways in which she could get him into trouble. Most part of Jaswinder Kaur's attitude towards Karamjit was because she had no son or daughter and she couldn't bear in mind that Karamjit would be the one who would take all the possessions and property that they have. This was the reason that she imprinted this hatred for Karamjit so intense in her heart that she couldn't resist herself from devising ways to do evil to him.

And Gurtej Singh lately came to know about this and even warned her for her actions but still couldn't get her in control as she behaved insolently to Karamjit.

5.
Big Moment

Karamjit was now in his last semester and just two weeks before his final exams of the 12th standard when his uncle Gurtej Singh asked to meet him in his room. Karamjit went to him and as he entered his uncle's room, he saw him sitting on his chair with some photos piled up on the table which he couldn't recognize from a distance. "Come, sit here" said Gurtej Singh as he slid the chair towards him. He sat down and Gurtej Singh kept looking at the pictures for another 5 minutes and then spoke, "You know Karamjit, your father and I were not only brothers but also very good friends. When we were younger, we would play together, go to parties together to look for girls and have a lot of fun together in our friend circle." he said as he paused for a second and then continued.

"But I never felt that he would leave me this soon. I miss him now. I wish I had some more time to talk to him and live like a child again and have all the fun that we had together. And that's why I have called you here, today. Because it's your time now. You are still young and you have a glorious life ahead waiting for you. So, it's not good for you to rely on things of the past and self-destruct in the process of doing so. I have made that mistake in my life and learned a lesson too which is the reason I am sharing this with you. Remember, it's always better to learn from mistakes of others than to commit them all by yourself. You understand that?" he asked

And Karamjit simply nodded his head in agreement. "So enjoy your youth to the fullest but make sure that you always consider the consequences before you make an important decision in your life. Because you don't live with the decision. You only make it momentarily. But you have to live your whole life with the consequences of the decision that you make. So be wise in this regard and take heed of my advice as it is to your best interest. I know, your aunt is a bit rude to you sometimes, but don't be bothered about that. She is getting soft with time and I have observed that. And you wouldn't want to know how she was 20 years ago!" They both laughed out as he said that.

" I had to share this thing which I have kept in my heart for so many years now. And I think now the right time has arrived where I can share it with you." "What are you talking about?" asked Karamjit. "It's a secret that was held from you by your father and he told me not to tell it to you until you grow up. But since he is no more, so I have to reveal it to you." "What is it?" "It's a will that your mother made to your father when she faced the accident while counting her last few breaths. You were still very young at that time. She laid on her death bed and while she was about to die, she whispered in your father's ears that she wanted you to grow up in The Bahamas." "What?" he interrupted.

" Not just that. You don't know this but your mother's grandparents used to live in the Bahamas decades ago. Your mother also was born in Bahamas and took her education and Masters degree from Bahamas University. After completing her education, she came and settled here in India with her old parents as the living conditions in the Bahamas were becoming very difficult for them at that time due to lack of proper resources and facilities. That grave condition of Bahamas was due to the independence they got from British rule in 1973 leaving them with a government of their own but no funds to keep the island thriving. They started living here and adapted themselves to the Indian culture and soon became citizens here.

She got a job in a consultation firm. Your father met her when he was deployed in a post in Pune. They got married and were living a settled and contended life when suddenly one day your mother met with a car accident while driving all alone by herself. She was hospitalized but the chances of her survival were scarce. And when she realized that her time on this planet was about to come to an end, she asked your father to let you visit the Bahamas and meet a person who teaches in the Bahamas University. Your father was listening to what she said but couldn't understand why she was saying that. He asked her what she meant but it was too late. Those were the last words that he heard from her as she left him.

"What did she meant?" asked Karamjit."Well, I don't know. The person that she wanted you to meet is Emmanuel Joshua. He was a Professor at the University at her time there and her mentor. That's all what she said" "It's eccentric" " I know, I know. And your father told this information to me about 5 years back and I hold it back from you as he told me to refrain from telling it to you till the right time comes. But I believe the right time has come now for you to know it so you can handle it in your own way." "So, does that mean, we are moving to the Bahamas?" asked Karamjit. "Not we..... but you" "What?" he exclaimed. "Yes, I have decided in a discussion with your aunt that since you are about to finish your 12th standard education soon, we will send you to the Bahamas on a study permit. You will do your degree there and that would also save us from any large expenses since you can get the degree without me spending plethora of money on your education. So it hits two birds with one arrow."

"But-But uncle, I have never been to another unknown place alone. How can I live there? I have never lived without you or father. If you want me to go the Bahamas, we can go there together please. That would be good for us." He pleaded. "Look Karamjit, I cannot leave India as I have some commitments with my army unit to serve them with my expertise and you know that I have to visit my battalion every twice a week. So it's not feasible for me to go with you. And moreover, you are grown up now. So, be a man and take some responsibility for yourself & move on with life." He said. "But uncle, I can't leave my friends. And where would I live there? We don't know anyone there. Right?" Karamjit tried to resist.

"Oh boy, you are certainly different as people say about you. Don't worry about your stay there. Your mother had a friend. His name is Mr. Richardson. They completed their degree together in the Bahamas. I also came to know about him through her when she was alive. I will contact him and he'll take care of your stay till you complete your education there. You will have to go the Bahamas and this is my order. I am not asking for your permission. I am telling you to prepare yourself to go there and it would be better if you could bid a good farewell to your friends. And that's why I am telling it to you quite well before time so that you could prepare yourself for it. Okay, enough for today. Now, go back to your room and sleep and I don't want any further discussion on this topic ever again. My command is final and you have to agree on that whether you like it or not" "Okay, good night." Karamjit murmured.

He went to his room and sat in front of monitor of his computer. He typed in Bahamas in Google Search and numerous images clicked in front of him. He read that the Bahamas was an archipelago of more than over 700 islands whose capital was Nassau. He came to know more that it was the University of the Bahamas that his uncle was talking about to him. As he researched more about the Bahamas, he felt excited by the environment and the beaches he saw. It seemed a good place to live for him but at the same time, he was also nervous as he had never travelled outside the country by himself before. And as he was a quiet guy, it would be difficult for him to live there all by himself. He thoughts of himself: this country seems to me a nice place with beaches and nice weather making it a perfect place to spend time but how am I going to survive there? Uncle does not have enough money to just spend on me, so how would I be able to manage the expenses. He began to calculate the expenses that he would have to incorporate to live in the Bahamas. Although Bahamas was not a blooming economy but still it has much more expenses than in India because of lack of the resources and their non-availability at some of the places in the island.

He went to sleep planning to talk about the matter to his friends Amrit and Riya. The very next day, he went to school and told Amrit about this. And Amrit was overly excited when he heard about it. " Oh, Wow! That's so exciting Karamjit." "Exciting? I think it's terrible to me" "Why do you say that? You know what, you are so lucky that you have got the opportunity to visit in a beautiful country like the Bahamas. Many desire to go into some other countries like Canada or Australia to study there. Out of every ten people here, six of them desire to leave the country and settle in another one. And you have got this golden opportunity and you are denying it? What's wrong with you?" "But I will have to leave you. Isn't that bad?" " It is, but your future is more important than this friendship. And a genuine friend would never forsake their friend's future for the sake of merely their friendship. So, I would suggest you to just grab this opportunity to get the most out of it. Do you understand that? And I want you to also tell Riya about this. I am sure she would encourage you to do the same." He added. "Umm.... Okay." Said Karamjit.

After that he met Riya and told her about her mother's last will and how his uncle asked him to leave India and go to the Bahamas. " Oh, that's great." She said although her face revealed something else. "Do you really want me to leave? " he asked. " Yeah, that's good for you." She said taking a deep breath. "Okay, so I must go" " You leaving?" she asked. " That's what you said. So you don't mean it? " " No... why would I care about that huh?" she said thinking for a second. " Okay, let's sit and talk for a while." And then he continued. "Look, I don't want to leave you but I have to because of my uncle's pressure. And moreover, we can always talk on the phone whenever we feel to do so.

No?" " Right" she answered. " Once I get my bachelor's degree from the Bahamas, I will return to India back." " So that's what you have planned?" she asked. " I mean, that's what my uncle has planned for me." She looked away in despair. "What time is it?" she asked. Karamjit looked at his Hungerford watch and said, "Its 3'o clock. Are you getting late?" "Not really. Just asking. By the way, I always wanted to you ask that your watch looks pretty expensive to me. Did someone gifted it to you?"

" Actually, this is a memory that I have always cherished. When I was 11 years old, during his posting in Fort William in Kolkata he had the opportunity to pick this watch up, and my father gifted it to me and since then I wear it everyday and whenever I look at it, it reminds me of the connection that I had with my father. And now when he is not with me, it reminds me even more of him. His words resonating in my mind and how he used to inspire me to keep moving in tough times. This watch is very close to my heart." "Nice. Which brand is it?" "It's called Hungerford. I just absolutely love this watch." " I can see that. I have never seen your wrist without that watch." She said. " Okay then, I think it's time for me to leave." " Uhh... alright. See you soon before I leave the country." He said as he saw her getting out of his sight feeling a strange sensation strongly which was about her and the psychological pain that he would have to suffer of losing her.

Many days went by and he finally completed his 12th standard exams with a decent score and then there was the day when he had to leave for the Bahamas. He called Amrit to see him for the last time and Riya too, but she didn't picked up his call even though he tried many times but failed. He asked Amrit to call her but in vain. It was time for his flight so he couldn't visit her house to see her. He bid a final farewell to Amrit as he got ready to leave for the airport.

" Take care buddy and call me whenever you have the time. " Said Amrit. " I will come back soon brother. You have been a true friend to me all this time and I cannot thank you enough for your generosity. Take care bro. I will talk to you soon once I reach there." He shook hands with him and then touched feet of his uncle and aunt which is a regular tradition in India. Whenever an individual leaves the elders or meets them, they show respect for them by touching their feet and taking their blessings with them. His aunt hugged him tightly while feeling happy inside that she finally has got rid of this clumsy boy and he would stay away from them for at least another 3 years. While his uncle Gurtej Singh folded his arms around his shoulders just like a friend would do and said, " All the best son, for your journey and always remember what I told you that night. Keep that in mind and never forget it. And once you reach there, I have asked Mr. Richardson who will pick you up from the airport and take you to the house that you have to live in. I have paid the rental for the next two months and will keep sending you the required money whenever you need it. You just inform me for whatever you need and I am always here for you." He said as he kissed Karamjit's forehead while he was about to get into the cab to leave for the Delhi airport from where he had to get his flight.

He sat in the cab and waved his hand at all of them as he bid them the final farewell and the cab moved on to take him to the Delhi airport. He started from Patiala at 8 a.m. in the morning and reached Delhi airport at six in the evening. He tried one last time to call Reya, who was with her parents in a hotel in Paharganj, New Delhi. The trip was about 40 minutes out from the airport, but he knew he couldn't afford to miss her.

Riya asked Karamjit to come up to her hotel room. What followed after that moment was a whirlwind of passion that carried the two into the private room while Riya's parents were out. It was Riya who initiated first, greeting him with a passionate kiss and seductive arm rubbing.

She welcomed him into that room. She was going to make him a man that night. It was the least she could do to show how much she loved him. Karamjit proved himself to be quite the animal from the get-go as the door to the room closed behind them and he had Riya pinned to the wall with his lips exploring every inch of her neck. "I want you to not hold back," she whispered to him. Riya wanted to prove she could be just as much an animal as she proceeded to reach for Karamjit's belt and pulled him closer to her body. "I give you permission to use my whole body."

Both of them stripped down at rapid speed as Riya was already moaning before Karamjit was completely naked. Before this moment, neither of them had seen each other in such a way and it called their attention to stare and behold the beauty of their naked bodies. Karamjit thrusted his body back up against Riya passionately as his hands grasped her freed breasts and the two reveled in the touch of each other's skin. She took in a heavy whiff of the masculine scent of Karamjit's musk as he grabbed hold of her. Karamjit then lifted her up with his strong arms and grasped her ass cheeks firmly. Riya wrapped her legs around Karamjit's thighs and thrusted her body into him, letting his dick press against her pulsating lips and her clit could feel every sensation of his rigid dick. The two continued to grind against each other until Karamjit whisked Riya off the wall and dropped her down on the bed with him on top of her.

Karamjit groaned with pleasure as he sat upon his knees and wrapped his arms around Riya's shoulders and thighs. Riya cooed with pleasure as she grabbed hold of his pulsating meat and pulled him into her mouth. She opened wide and gleefully invited him inside as she caressed his foreskin with her tongue and clamped her lips down hard around his shaft so she could suck. Karamjit let out a pleased groan as he pushed his fingers up against her muff and rubbed them around her lips and clitoris. Riya moaned onto Karamjit's dick as she had become swollen from how turned on she was to fuck such an animal in bed. Karamjit started to pick up speed with his hand as he gyrated his wrist and pumped two fingers into her. Riya gasped with pleasure as she pushed back and arched her legs. She started to moan louder and louder as Karamjit persisted with his aggressive fingering.

Her yelps turned into cries as she convulsed with pleasure and let out a loud, powerful orgasmic scream. "I really want you to go all the way," she said. "I don't want you to hold back those primal instincts."

"I'll make you feel like a woman, my love," said Karamjit with a smirk.

He grasped both of Riya's breasts in hand and squeezed them. Her nipples stood up on end as he generously suckled on them, alternating every so often just to watch Riya squirm. He moved his hands slowly down her body once more and pushed his wet fingers back into her. Riya gasped in excitement as she looked at him. The sound of his fingers as they pushed through a flowing river of cum echoed throughout the room. Both of them tried their damn best to keep quiet, seeing as they were in a semi-public space. The exhilarating feelings that drove them were just too much. Riya had to smother her mouth to stop from screaming as she laid back on the bed with her legs open. Karamjit huffed like an animal trying to subdue himself before he went too wild. He was enamored by her beauty and the moment was just too hot and heavy to hold back. She thrusted her body against his fingers and grabbed at his neck to support her body as she arched back.

Her second orgasm was loud and fast as she screamed relentlessly. Karamjit didn't have to think twice as he held Riya up in the air by her ass. He pushed his face down into her wet lips and licked up from her vagina to her engorged clitoris. Riya convulsed again as she winced from the amount of consistent orgasming she was experiencing. Karamjit enjoyed the taste of her wetness as he lapped it up like a dog. Her cum was succulent sweet and it lubricated her inner walls to the point that his tongue merely glided along her inner walls. Riya pleaded in a more incoherent jargon as the teasing was all too much for her. Finally, Karamjit gave in and dropped her body back on the bed, grabbed his dick in hand, and easily slid himself deep inside her. Riya cried out in orgasmic pleasure as she wrapped her legs around Karamjit's waist. She was so overwhelmed with emotion that she couldn't control her thoughts anymore, all she could think about was how much she wanted him to ravish her.

"There is a condom you can use," she whispered, pointing to the end table.

Like a good boy, he grabbed it and hastily put it on, stopping only for a moment to understand how it worked before he figured it out. Karamjit proceeded to thrust vigorously into her wetness with ease as she cried in pleasure. She held her legs out and let her feet dangle in the air as Karamjit's body slapped against hers. He breathed out heavily in pleasure as he could feel Riya's walls tightened on his dick. The lubrication from her cum made it easy for him to force his way in as deep as possible. He arched his legs up and pushed down on Riya's legs until they pressed against the mattress. Riya gasped as she looked up at Karamjit. He didn't realize how incredibly flexible she was and from the look on her face, she didn't realize either. She had never been handled so roughly yet so passionately by a fleeting lover. She whimpered with pleasure as she struggled to breathe. Her body being scrunched back made the feeling of Karamjit's dick even more fulfilling. Karamjit could feel his head punch against Riya's cervix from how deeply he thrusted into her. Of course she loved every moment of his thrusting.

Riya screamed hard, her voice cracking as she only received air after every upward thrust Karamjit made. She held her legs up in the air as her thighs hugged his body. Karamjit grasped his hands around her feet and clenched them tightly as he further pushed down on her body.

Their thighs clapped against each other in a heavy rhythmic motion as Karamjit continued to fuck with great intensity. He pinned Riya down as she sunk further and further into the bed before she gasped and straightened her legs from another intense orgasm. Karamjit pulled back off of her and breathed out. He stood up on his knees as he watched Riya struggle to turn around and present herself.

She was barely able to make it to her knees before he had to grab her by the waist and prop her up in front of him. He grabbed her cheeks and spread open her vagina as he caressed his shaft between the soft, throbbing lips. Riya's knees gave in as she buckled from the sheer intensity of her pleasure. Karamjit used his strength to hoist her back up into position as he pushed himself deep inside her. From the new position, she felt even tighter as she cooed pleasantly from the new feeling. He growled more than groaned, which didn't seem too odd to Riya as he seemed more like an animal than a mere man. It only served to turn her on even more, feeling him ravish her so primitively.

Karamjit held firm to Riya's waist as he grabbed her hair with his free hand and pulled it back. Riya gasped from the rough handling she was receiving and loved every second of it. Now she was on her knees in a submissive doggy-style. "Look at you, so forceful," she cooed.

Karamjit started to thrust slower this round as he took his time in each calculated rhythmic motion. He focused on the tightness of Riya's vagina as it clasped firmly around his shaft. He pushed in slowly as he let go of her waist and let her body push against his. He reached around and proceeded to rub on her clitoris as Riya punched the mattress and gasped. "Oh yes, you do me so good," she moaned as she tripped on her words, shaking her body against him.

"That's because you are everything to me," chuckled Karamjit as he whispered to her seductively. "And I want you to always remember this moment."

It was clear that Karamjit had given her more than she ever expected. He was even impressed with himself at this point. It was also clear to Riya that this sort of love-making was more her speed than the simple, tender loving she often received. As much as she could appreciate the soft tenderness and would like to feel it again, there was something about this rough ravishing that was revitalizing her spirit. She pushed her face into the blankets and screamed several times over as Karamjit sped up his thrusting. She turned her head and breathed out.

"I'm about to explode," whispered Karamjit. "Should I pull out?"

She shook her head no. She didn't want this moment to end. She continued to hold on to him and clench her thighs tightly, refusing to let go. He pumped and pumped and huffed and huffed as he thrusted. It was then that it dawned on him that this was the moment. This was the climax. He wasn't a virgin anymore and he was about to finish with Riya. She grabbed him by the back of the neck and pulled him in for a passionate kiss as the two continued to grind against each other, feeling the sweet release flow out of them in unison. Riya moaned into his mouth as she came just as he did with her. He felt her body tighten and work his dick until he was completely spent. He gasped and pulled away, lying next to her on the bed and removing the condom.

"I can not believe it escalated that quickly," he said to her, looking down at himself then at her. He took her hand and breathed out slowly. "I will remember this... this was beautiful."

"You were brilliant," she chuckled.

"But you were the conductor," he responded. "I don't know if I could have become such a man like that if it wasn't for you."

They shared several more long passionate kisses before finally Karamjit had to force himself up to get dressed. Her parents were returning soon and he had a flight to catch. The pleasantries could have lasted all night if he chose to. Sadly, he and Riya had to part ways. They shared tearful goodbyes before Karamjit set out to catch another taxi heading back to the airport.

He went through all the security procedures at the airport and started waiting eagerly in the waiting room for his flight to take off. He had his ticket in hand. He was sitting there idle, so he started reading the information written on the ticket. He saw that the journey was from New Delhi to Nassau, which is the capital of the Bahamas. The name of the Airline was 'United Airlines' with a ticket number UA-899 which was to depart at 10'o clock which would then arrive at Nassau airport the other day at eight in the evening.

He kept looking at the strange faces at the airport and felt a little discomfort. He wasn't even there in the flight yet and started feeling sick. It was his fear of going out alone. He started feeling nervous about what will happen next as this was the first time he set out on a journey to another country by himself alone. Due to this nervousness, he started double-checking everything that he brought with himself in his bag. He checked his passport, he checked his phone, checked another identity proof. Everybody who looked at him could sense his insecurity by the way he acted.

Then finally the clock was about to struck ten when he went to board the plane. He sat in the Economy class. He listened to all the instructions that the flight attendants gave him and then followed them rigorously. And as soon as flight took off, he felt a jerk as he leaned back to his seat. This made his heart beat even faster. He felt like asking someone for help but when the plane reached to a certain height, he started feeling comfortable with it. He looked out of the window and all he could see was clouds below him.

He took a magazine which was kept on the back cover the front seat and started reading it. On the magazine were pictures of beautiful beaches and he started imagining one of them to be in the Bahamas. He imagined himself travelling in the sunny weather of Bahamas and chilling out in the exotic beaches. He got lost in his imagination when suddenly he woke up and a beautiful Air hostess was standing next to him. "Do you want something to eat for the breakfast Sir?" she asked with a genuine smile. " No. I don't feel like eating anything right now. Thanks for asking. But can you please get a water bottle for me?" he asked. " Sure Sir, I will just get it in a minute. Do you want anything else?" " Nothing else. Thanks" he said. He took the water bottle and drank nearly half a litre of water to get refreshed. He looked at his Hungerford watch which struck twelve. He went to sleep again only to wake up in the evening just before the flight was about to arrive at the Nassau Airport.

The plane arrived at the Nassau Airport at the expected timing. He took his luggage off the counter and stepped out of the Airport. He saw a man standing in the waiting lane holding a Play card in his hands on which was written 'KARAMJIT SINGH From India' in bold letters. He immediately got to know that this is the person that his uncle Gurtej Singh was talking about. The man was tall and big almost twenty centimeters taller than him. He went to him and told him his name and the man shook hands with him and said that his name was Mr. Richardson and showed Karamjit the way to his car where they sat and took off for their destination. Karamjit was sitting quiet all this while and Mr. Richardson could easily figure it out that he was an introvert.

" Tell me something about you, Karamjit? " he asked as he took a sharp left from the highway joining the airport. " Umm... I am here to get a bachelor's degree in Business and Administration from The University of The Bahamas " " So what are your interests?" he asked. " Uhh... I like to spend time with my friends, visit Gurudwara and some gardening. That's all I used to do in my spare time in India." " I see that you have never travelled by yourself eve r in your whole life and your shy nature is a proponent for that. But anyhow, doesn't matter. Since you are here now, I would suggest you to be very open minded. I have had some friends who used to live in India. And observing them I can very well say that they too were just like you; shy and introvert. But all of them have become good communicators now and doing well in their respective areas of competence. I am sure you will reflect on that too." He paused for a second and looked at Karamjit's face and then continued.

" You see Karamjit, I have never met you before and I figured you out in just two minutes that you don't speak much and are reluctant to speak up your mind to others. But you see, you can live the way you want when you have someone to care for you. But when you come to live in another country all by yourself, you become responsible for yourself and you cannot survive here in this culture if you don't speak up for yourself. People will eat you alive. I know that because I have been living here as a citizen for the last twenty years. Gurtej Singh and I have been very good friends since last couple of years as I met him through your mother during my visit in India. Your mother and I graduated from Bahamas University in the same batch, if you know. She was a good friend and that is why I am advising you. It will become difficult for you to survive like that forget about thriving in these challenging times with grinding competition in the market and the globalization has even made it worse. Do you understand what I am saying or am I just talking to myself? " he asked as he took a look at Karamjit.

" Yes, Sir. I do understand what you are talking about." he responded almost immediately nodding his head. " Then please do give me response. I am telling this to you because I don't want my friend's son to suffer in this hard economy." He said. He kept driving for another one hour after which he said, " Okay Karamjit, we are about to reach to our destination. Get yourself ready."

He stopped the car in an alley. Karamjit unbuckled his seat belt and stepped out of the car. As he stepped out, he saw that the place was full of dirt and mud everywhere around that place. Manholes were kept open and stray dogs were eating the mud sprinkled on the ground. Karamjit looked a bit scared looking at the dogs and Mr. Richardson saw it. " Don't worry about those Potcake Dogs. They are loyal and intelligent. They'll get to recognize you soon as you spend some time here." Said Mr. Richardson. As he turned around, he saw a small apartment. " This is the place where you will live Karamjit. Let's go and take a look inside. Take your luggage with you." Said Mr. Richardson. Karamjit took his luggage with a bag on his shoulders and walked towards the house carefully stepping on the ground protecting his shoes and pants from getting dirty from the foeces of the dogs.

Mr. Richardson knocked on the door, a feeble voice came back. " Wait, please. Coming..." and after a minute the door opened in a slow manner and an old woman's face was the first thing that he saw. The woman was rather short about five feet tall probably in her seventies. The woman lifted her head up to look at Mr. Richardson who was looking a giant in comparison to her. " Yes?" she asked. " Hello Mrs. Olsen, how are you doing now? It's been quite a long time. Right?" " Yes, dear. I am doing great even at this stupendous age. How did you remember me after such a long time Richardson? The last time you visited me was about a year back I suppose."

" Ahh... yes. You know the pressure of work doesn't allow a man to spend some time with a beautiful lady like you. It's not my fault and you know that." " Come inside please." She said. " Come Karamjit" said Mr. Richardson. " By the way, who is this young man, Richard?" she asked as she pointed her finer towards Karamjit. " Ahh... I forgot to tell you that he is coming. This is the boy that I talked to you. He is from India and he is here to get a bachelor's degree from The University of The Bahamas. You remember? I told you about him on the phone." He asked.

" Oh.... Now I remember. You see, this is the predicament of the old age. You never know when you forget even little things so easily. Old age really sucks Richardson." " Ahhmm.. I know that. I can feel your pain." Said Mr. Richardson in a witty tone.

" No, you don't Richardson. You are still in your fifties. You are young and healthy. So, don't pretend that you understand the pain that this old lady is going through. Okay? And I have warned you many times before, not to try your sarcasm on me. I think you will learn it the hard way. Don't you?"

" Ha- ha- ha. I was just kidding. Don't get too serious about that Mrs. Olsen. You are just like my mother. And that's why I respect you so much. I have spent almost half of my life with you, that's why I care for you so much." " Okay, okay. I know that. Don't be so cheesy now. I am making some hot tea for both of you. By the way, what is the name of this young man?" " He is Karamjit Singh. You can simply call him Karamjit or Sardarji. That would be even better." " Okay then. Karamjit, tell me something about you please." She asked. "Uhh...." He hesitated while Mr. Richardson interrupted. " Actually he don't speak a lot. And while I was driving him here, I told him that it's necessary for him to speak to be heard. Otherwise, people won't treat him right. That's good advice. Right Mrs. Olsen?"

" Yeah. I mean, who could give better advice on speaking than you huh? You can't stop talking all the time, you always want to say something just for the sake of saying it. Do you want to be humiliated more?" she said. Karamjit kept there sitting on the dining table sipping his tea listening to them talk so compassionately with a little bit of wit and humor reflecting the connection they both had with each other.

As they finished the tea, Mrs. Olsen told Mr. Richardson to take Karamjit with him and show him the room where he will live. "Come upstairs Karamjit" said Mr. Richardson as he stepped up the stairs.

Karamjit followed him. Mr. Richardson opened the door of the room and dust sprinkled outside the room as the door opened. Sharp light came from the window in the corner of the room. There was some furniture piled up with bed sheets folded up near a fragile bed. The floor was all dusty and dirty with a strong smell which messed both of their senses. They covered up their noses.

" I think some work needs to be done in this room to make it clean. We can get the worker to clean the room until tomorrow. Meanwhile, you can stay in the basement for today Karamjit. Will that be okay for you?" he asked. " Yes, it would work for me." " The only problem in the basement is that there is no faculty for air conditioning and not even a fan. And the temperature is very hot. So you will have to manage to stay there for today somehow." " No worries. I will manage it. After all, it's just for one day." After which, Mr. Richardson bid farewell to Mrs. Olsen and left in his car for his business trips to come back to her the next year. That was all that Karamjit knew about the life of Mr. Richardson.

Karamjit went to the basement and stuffed up his luggage there. There was no bed for him to sleep. So he took some bed sheets from the room and laid them on the ground and rested there for some time. He was tired after a long and arduous journey. He started thinking of Amrit and Riya. He was even amazed that he still has not encountered any problems in this journey which was not so usual for him. He even anticipated for some bad things to happen to him as it was the part of his life that he couldn't get away without encountering a bad circumstance which would rip him apart. All that was normal for him and he even had constructed this mindset where he would wake up every day and anticipate some really terrible things to happen to him.

He thought of calling Riya and Amrit to gather his emotions together. He called Riya at first but she didn't pick up his call. He became a little skeptic and worried as she also didn't picked up his call when he was about to leave his home. He started thinking: what could be the reason for her not picking up my phone? Is she okay? Or is she just upset about the fact that I left her and came to the Bahamas? He started gathering a bunch of emotions about it. Then he called Amrit and luckily Amrit picked up his call.

"Hey Karamjit, have you reached that place Bro? Tell me about your journey. Oh.. I am so excited for you." Said Amrit. " Yes Amrit, the journey was fine for me and I met Mr. Richardson, the person that uncle talked about and he took me in his car to this apartment where I am staying right now which is owned by an old lady named Mrs. Olsen. The room in which I have to stay is actually quite filthy right now, so until it gets sorted out I am living in the basement for now." " Great. So tell me about the weather. How is the weather? Is it too hot there?" " Well... it's really hot in here. Even though I haven't been out. I came here straight through the car but still I can feel my whole body sweating as I am speaking to you now. The place where I am living right now is called the Bain Town. It's close to the Capital Nassau." " What about the University where you will study. When will its session begin?" " Maybe in the next month or so. I am not really sure about its opening. They say you will get a notification when the academic session starts. All the fee for the education is paid for. The rent for this apartment is paid for the next two months. So, I don't think there is anything left to worry about."

" Sounds cool. So you will be enjoying the cool breeze with the sunset on the beach. Don't you? " Ha Ha. Sure. That's on my bucket list. That would be kind of normal here" " Alright. Have you talked to Riya?" " No, I haven't. I don't know why but she is not picking up my phone since I left home. Do you know anything about her?" "Well, she left with her family about two days ago in their jeep somewhere and haven't come back yet. Maybe they've gone to some weekend trip as her father had some government holidays issued to him." " I see. Okay, just let me know when you talk to her and inform her that I wanted to talk to her." " You getting so desperate Huh?" Amrit said jokingly. " Hey, come on man. Be serious sometimes. Okay, I will get back to you later." He said as he hung up the phone.

He laid down back on the ground over the bed sheets and took some rest until the evening. When he woke up, he heard a knock on the door. He opened the door and saw Mrs. Olsen standing at the door. " Yes Mrs. Olsen?" he asked. " Come Karamjit, the meal is ready. Freshen up yourself and come on the dinning table. Let's eat the dinner." " At this time?" he questioned. " What do you mean 'at this time'?" " I mean, isn't it too early to eat dinner. It's only seven." " We eat our dinner at this time. It's good for you to eat early and then go to bed early. So, if you want to stay here, you have to follow the rules. We can't cook separately for you on your desired time. Getting it?" "Coming then...." he said in a lowly voice.

Karamjit went to the main room where he ate his dinner. The food was cooked hot and he could almost smell the beautiful fragrance coming from the meat with hot sauce all over it. He ate the dinner making sure his stomach was full and then went straight away to the basement to sleep. The next day, his room was cleaned up and now he shifted to the room which was way better than living in the heat of the basement. All day, he would just keep laying there thinking about Riya. This routine continued for him day after day without breaks.

6.

The Commencement....

After about one month, it was time for him to join The University of The Bahamas. He got the notification on his email that the academic session has been started and all the students who have applied for intake in the university must come up on the very first day for the inaugural ceremony of the academic session. Karamjit was nervous and excited all at the same time. He would constantly think about the people that he would encounter at the University. And then get worried thinking if the people that he meet there would be exactly like the bullies that he faced in Patiala. But then he would remind himself of his father which encouraged him to think of not quitting and rather embracing difficulties and hardships as part of life.

And finally the day came when it was time for him to visit the University. It was the first day of the academic session. He got up early, washed his face and bathed. After which he ate his breakfast and dressed up in a casual manner just as he would dress up at his home in Patiala. He came out of the apartment, shut the door, and took the cab to reach university. " Can you take me to The University of The Bahamas please?" he asked the cab driver. " Sure. Please sit." He said. " It seems to me that you have come from another country to study here" " How do you know that?" he questioned.

" Well, I can say that just by looking at the way you politely asked me to drop you. People are quite discourteous in the Bahamas especially in the Bain town. Only outsiders talk in such courteous manner." " I have seen that also. Even the owner of the house which I am renting is rude and impolite. She is old but doesn't seem that she has any experience to deal with people in the right manner." " So what are you going to pursue in the University?" " I am going for the Bachelor's degree in Business and Administration" "Have you researched about the university before you joined it?" "Not quite well. I saw a thing or two. Can you tell me something about it? You must be knowing about it very well."

" Well.... I also graduated from that university, so I know it quite well. Basically, it's a liberal arts university and you can enroll in almost any program of every interest, from business and biology to engineering, whether it be theology, or law. One thing I can tell you for sure; when you get inside, you will certainly be amazed by the amazing architecture that it has. I mean, it's one of the best that you could ever perceive....." he stopped as he saw Karamjit feeling a bit low. Then he continued, "Seems like you are tired. You can take a nap if you want. It will take another 15 minutes to reach there. I will wake you up once we reach there." " No, I am good" said Karamjit.

After travelling for about ten minutes, he reached the university. All this while, he couldn't relax but instead he was getting nervous every passing second. So he couldn't realize when he reached there and the cab driver had to wake him up to his senses. He thanked the driver for letting him know. He stepped out of the cab. The cab left and as he turned around, he saw a big rounded stone one which was written "The University of The Bahamas" and as he moved a little further, he saw a huge architecture which was carved to shape into the hands of a praying man. It was called the praying hands.

The campus was humongous. Everywhere Karamjit could see, there were trees and plants and gardens all spread throughout the vast expanse of the campus. The round stone carving just besides the praying hands had an inverted triangle with a man in between. Around it was written: "mind, body and spirit signifying the connection between the three elements which make up a whole man or woman". As he moved ahead a hundred meters, he saw a building which was called the 'Praying Tower'.

As he was rummaging through the campus, he saw a large crowd gathered around a stage which was the auditorium in the open ground of the university where the director the university had to deliver the opening ceremony speech to which many people were waiting in anticipation to hear it and get a piece of mind of the director and the vision and mission of the university. There were some elderly people sitting on the chairs waiting for the ceremony to start.

He went to the place and sat down grabbing a chair for himself as he saw a number of white and black people preparing the stage for the ceremony to begin. He looked around and saw that the campus was packed with students. As he sat there and heard other people talk, he came to realize that he was not the only one who had come from a different country to study there. In fact, there were plethora number of people who came from other countries like Japan, Russia and even U.S. He learned from hearing people talk that most of them have come to study here because of the Bahamas tourism industry. The Bahamas's major source of revenue came from tourism industry and it was no surprise to him why they spend most of their money to attract more tourist which was their major source of revenue.

Soon, the seats in the auditorium started to fill up and the narrator started narrating about the history of the university and how it originated, telling more about its prominence and how it has helped millions of students time and again to live a satisfactory life and deliver to their expectations. After the narrator spoke for about ten minutes, he invited the director to come on the podium to deliver his speech. Suddenly, he could hear a loud applause from the audience most of which were students as the director arrived on the podium.

He began his speech by clearing his throat, " Ladies and Gentlemen, I am honored to have this opportunity year after another to deliver my thoughts to all the individuals like you who have come from many different countries to learn from this prominent university. You know that we are a multicultural campus with students representing many different countries bringing with them their talents and gifts which further help us to nurture them and refine them in their areas of competence. We offer our students not only academic excellence but also develop in them spiritual practices which helps them to find themselves so that they could become much more effective in whatever they choose to do in their life. Our mission and purpose is to produce better individuals with certain beliefs, attitudes and values that can spread in the whole community of like-minded people and create a chain of change which would help us make the world a better place to live. And we are going to do it through all of you. You are the individuals who are going to form the foundation for the manifestation of great ideas, inventions, books, and business that can impact millions of lives of people. Those people are waiting for you to manifest your gifts and talents to serve the world what you truly carry within you. We are glad that you have made the right choice of coming to this place to get equipped mentally, physically and spiritually which would not only help you to achieve your aspirations and the deepest desires of your heart but also let you make a difference to other people's life with your life............" the director continued on with his speech.

Meanwhile, Karamjit got bored with the long speech that the director was delivering. He moved his attention to the campus of the university to find something interesting. Everywhere that he could see, he only saw trees and gardens with some buildings and around one of them was the library which was rectangular whose foundation was narrow but it widened as it moved upwards. He perceived the library to be his confinement as it was against his very basic nature to talk to some strangers without any strong necessity. So he thought he could probably hide somewhere in the calmness of the library and wouldn't have to face the people out there. That would later prove to be a bad idea for him.

After some time, the director finished giving his speech as everyone else started applauding him, he copied them to become part of the group. After the ceremony, he heard the announcement from the presenter that the classes for the business and administration would be starting from the very next day. After which, he gave the details to the fresher's about the campus and the sports facility, then the library building and the commemorative hall. The speaker ended his description and Karamjit got up from his chair and hurried straight towards the exit to reach the apartment hoping he wouldn't have to talk to other people out there.

He believed if some one talks to him and he couldn't answer them in the right way, he would end up belittling himself in front of everybody else and become a subject of criticism just like it happened with him in Patiala. So he avoided meeting with people all this while. He was still insecure in his thinking considering himself inferior than others in terms of his ability to persuade others to do something with his communication skills. He took the cab and went to the apartment. When he arrived, he felt better. This was the moment that he was turning back to that old Karamjit who was afraid to talk to somebody that he never met before.

He thought that when he started living the Bahamas, it would change his circumstances but it was not so for him as he still was around people who were assertive and in some ways dominative. It was partly because of Karamjit's inability to raise his voice when there was a need to do so. There was some fault on his own part that he never spoke for himself and never clearly expressed his intention of what he wanted from people that were around him. This habit of his even worsened the matter much more than ever.

He would just sit alone in his room in the darkness afraid to go out and mingle with others. Even though he had thought many times before about going to some of the prominent beaches in the Bahamas but he had a complexion of rejection which never allowed him to do that. He always feared that since he was a very fragile guy, people could bully him easily like they did in India. And so, he would normally avoid people. He would rarely talk to Amrit now and he failed to contact Riya even though he tried it before many times. The next day he went to the university, the campus was even more crowded than it was on the opening day. His heart started pounding as he walked inside the campus building slowly gathering himself trying to look confident but his slouching posture could easily reveal to anyone who observed him that he was terribly afraid.

He would simply go straight to his class where the first lecture was by the Accounting Professor Braid Williams followed by a lecture on Business Economics by Professor Nathan which was then backed up by a lecture on Marketing Management by Professor Wellington. Karamjit would keep sitting in the course although, he couldn't understand a word sometimes uttered by the lecturer which made him even more frustrated at his situation. He would go hide in the library in the brakes between the lectures and after all of them were finished, he would go run straight to the apartment where he would keep sitting alone for hours without ever going outside. He would eat his meal when Mrs. Olsen would call her. But he wouldn't talk to her even though she would keep telling him the stories of her youth and how she made a tough living coming from a very modest family background. Karamjit would listen to all she would say but not utter a single word other than just nodding his head in agreement whenever she looked to him for approval.

One day, his uncle Gurtej Singh called him to ask him about his well-being. He picked up the call and greeted him. " Hello uncle" " Yes, yes. Hello Karamjit. How are you my Son? It's been quite a long time since you called me here." Said Gurtej Singh. " I am doing well Uncle. I hope you and aunt are good too. Actually, I was busy since the university session has already begun and there's a lot of pressure of studies so I had to focus my attention to studies. That's why I couldn't call you."

" No worries boy. Just keep grinding hard. If there are any issues regarding anything, just let me know if I can help. Just call me whenever you need my help. Don't even think twice before calling me. Even though you are grown up now, but it's still my responsibility to make sure you enjoy your stay there. I am sending you the money for your rent payment. The two month period is about to end. So, withdraw it from your account and pay it before it gets late. You see, people there are a whole lot different there. They won't let you stay in the apartment even if you miss the payment by a single day. They are more concerned about acquiring materialistic possessions than about making healthy long lasting relationships. So please make sure you keep a vigilant eye on who you associate with. Don't spoil yourself with people of questionable character. Okay?" he asked. " No, uncle. I don't even go anywhere outside the apartment I am living in. So there's no way I can get along with wrong people." " I was just reminding you to be very protective of who you allow to get into your head. Getting it or not?" " I will keep an account of that. Don't worry please." He paused for a second and then said, " Okay, uncle. I will talk to you later. I have to eat my dinner now" and he immediately cut off the call and went to Mrs. Olsen's dining table to eat his dinner at the same time listen to her never ending stories of her youth.

Two days passed and Karamjit withdrew the money that his uncle sent him. And as he was passing through an alley and counting the notes, some men came on two motorbikes. He turned around to see and suddenly they reached closer to him and grabbed the money from his hands and raced away. He shouted but the alley was completely deserted. He ran after them with all his strength utilizing his stamina but in vain, their bikes were too fast for him to catch them. After chasing them for some hundred meters, he got tired and stopped to gasp some air.

His knees felt weak as he felt powerless to do anything. He stood there absolutely helpless. It was the money which would have paid his rent. He thought to himself: what should I do now? Should I tell uncle about this incident and ask him to send more money? No-No- No. That would not be good at all. It's not good to trouble him with that. But what can I do other than that? I will be thrown out of the apartment without paying the rent.

He continued to walk to the apartment thinking he would somehow try to convince Mrs. Olsen about the matter and do some of her household work in return of the rent money. He came back to apartment and went to Mrs. Olsen's room and told her about the incident. " So what?" she said almost immediately. " Can I do some of your work in turn of the rent money Mrs. Olsen? Please?" he asked politely. " Look, young man. If I had some work to do for you, I would have asked you before. Since I already have a maid and a cook, I am afraid you will have to take your luggage with you and leave the room." " What if I can find a job to pay your rent? Would that be fine? Can you please give me some time to find a job to pay your rent? That would be really helpful." He asked. " Alright. But I give you a week to find some work to do but at the end of that week, I want my rental payment and if you are not able to make some money then I shouldn't have to tell you again to leave the room. Do you understand that?" " Okay, I will do something..." he murmured.

He then called Amrit and told him how his money got stolen looking for some sympathy from Amrit. But instead, Amrit started yelling at him, " What are you doing Karamjit? Oh, man. When are you going to learn huh? When will you become more responsible and active in your social life? I warned you several times before as well. Now, live with the consequences." " But Amrit...." He spoke but got interrupted. "But....

But what huh?" " But it could have happened with almost anybody. The situation is even worse here. The place I live here, most of the people are criminals living in the alleys where it's almost impossible to get them. How can anyone live in such a place where there is no trust and security bestowed upon us? That's unfair" he said. Amrit took a deep breath trying to calm himself down.

"Look Karamjit, the world is not so innocent as you are. Everybody is not like you and don't even expect others to be like you. If you are expecting them to be like you, you are setting yourself up for disappointment. Okay now do one thing, I have heard that you can easily find a cleaning job there. You told me that the there is a lot of mess on the streets in the Bain Town. Right?" " There certainly is" he replied. "Great. So you can ask people to clean the dirt in their locality. I am sure there would be many people who would be frustrated about the messy streets but won't be doing anything about it. So you can do it for them" " But that's below me" he shouted.

" Do you think you are in a position to talk of what's below you and what is not? It's the only way I see to resolve your problem. If you want my take on that, that's it right there. Go for it and don't think too much of the ramifications of doing it. Just hit it right now if you don't want any further trouble for yourself" Said Amrit. " Alright, I will get started from tomorrow onwards but I will have to manage my timings of the university as well. It's going to be tiring as I am already travelling a lot from apartment to university and back again." " But that's the only way. Just remember who your inspiration is." " Yeah, that's my dad. Thanks for reminding it to me again. I will get something done soon. Bye"

The next day he woke up and went to the university to attend his classes and then rushed back to the apartment after that. After which he finally got out of the apartment for the first time for a purpose other than just withdrawing money. He knocked on every door in the street next to the alley. He asked people if they wanted to get the dirt in the street sorted out. Most of them rejected him saying they have no time to even talk to him. Some ignored him. But some actually paid him to get the streets cleaned up. And at the end of the day, he was all greasy with dirt but he also earned some bucks which gave him some hope of not losing the apartment.

He went to Mrs. Olsen and showed her the money that he earned. " But that's not okay for me." She said. " You have to keep earning every day, only then you would gather enough money to pay your rent. Don't think I will be lenient towards you because you are young. You are simply a regular guy to me who pays rent and uses the resources in this house. That's it " " I will surely pay your rent. But please don't throw me away. I have nowhere else to go. I don't even know anybody here." " Well, that's your problem. But as long as you are paying the rent, I don't care what you do, you can stay here" she left for her room saying that. And Karamjit picked up the money and went marching towards his room with a crushed spirit.

He had never thought that he would be washing dishes and cleaning dirt of other people's houses to pay some money to an old woman. He would continue doing that everyday even though he was getting frustrated every passing day with the way his life was going on. There seemed no way for him to break out of his rut and live a life that he dreamt of living. Every time he thought he is out of the trouble, something much terrible would strike him and leave him devastated. This was becoming a normal part of his living and the sad part for him was that he accepted this condition to be normal and never thought of getting through it by doing something that he has never done before.

7.
Misery Continues

Karamjit's life continued in the same manner for the next one month. He would clean streets, houses, and wash dishes to get some money for his rent. And he was successfully paying it after every week without ever missing a single payment. That gave him some relief that at least he is not a burden to his uncle now by being able to manage his own expenses. He would earn sufficient money which would save him some bucks even after paying his rent. One day, while he was coming back after attending his class, a shrill voice stopped him from behind.

" Hey dude, can you stop for a second?" it said. Karamjit stood there afraid to turn around until the man who had called him came to him. " Where are you heading to?" " Why should I tell you?" said Karamjit. " Boy, you are very eccentric. Do you know that I am in your class? It's been three months for you in this university and since the time I have been observing you, I have never seen you talk to anyone. You are quiet in the lectures after which you straight away leave the campus without mingling with anyone. Is everything okay with you or is it just that you talk less with strangers?" " I am good. Thank you. I don't need your help." "Woah ... dude. You are being too rude. Listen, me along with my friends can hang out with you if you feel lonely. What's the matter huh? Tell me." " Please leave my way. I have to leave for home" said Karamjit. And he left as soon as he finished saying it.

The next day, while he was sitting in the lecture room, the same guy came to him and sat next to him. Karamjit's posture began to fall down as if he was almost going down the chair on which he was sitting. Some other bunch of boys and girls came with that guy. " Hey guys, this is the person I was talking about" he said. " What's your name dude?" he asked. "What do you want with my name?" " Calm down dude, why are you hyper all the time? I am just asking your name." he said. "Karamjit" he responded. " Guys, meet Karamjit." He said to his friends as everybody started waving at him. "Karamjit, these are my friends. I am Nile from Haiti." He said and then started introducing every one of his friends to Karamjit.

Karamjit felt comfortable now as he perceived no threat from those people. " So are you free today? Maybe we can have some fun in the cafeteria together." Nile asked. " Well, I don't have to do anything specific for today but....." " Well, that's great then. Let's meet in the cafeteria after the lecture." Said Nile as he interrupted Karamjit. "But what are we going to do in the cafeteria?" " Umm... Nothing specific. We will have our lunch and talk some politics, some sports, some general issues. That would give us a clear picture of what's going on around us." " So, is it a kind of group discussion?" " You can say so. Discussions are a good way to sort out some uncluttered things in your mind and we generally do it to get rid of our old ways of thinking. You know, to think in a creative way. To get the things done in a new and unprecedented way. Hope you are getting it. Haven't you talked to any stranger before? Don't mind Karamjit but it seems to me that you are into yourself all the time, hasn't anyone pointed out that to you before?" he asked. " A lot of them did actually. But doesn't matter to me. I am the way I am. And I believe if someone really likes you, they would accept you the way you are. So I don't have any unrealistic expectations from anyone either. I mind my own business and I expect others to do the same." " You are surely different man. Okay, the lecture is about to start. But anyhow, as I said, come to the cafeteria after the lecture and I'll see you there." Said Nile.

As the lecture finished, Karamjit was about to leave for his apartment when all of a sudden Nile shouted from behind. "Hey Karamjit, don't run away. I told you to come to cafeteria, where are you going now?" " Can we talk some other day?" he asked. " Do you have to do something important today?" " Not really. But...." "Then no but. Come, let's get to know one another better." Said Nile as he hold Karamjit's hand and dragged him alongside to the cafeteria. They sat down on the chair for some time and after about two minutes, some of Nile's friends also joined them. Karamjit as usual felt uncomfortable in large groups of people. " Can I leave now, please?" he asked. " We have just come here, Karamjit. Okay, tell us something about you." Asked Nile.

And slowly and hesitatingly, Karamjit began to give him a description of himself. His early life In Patiala, his friends Riya and Amrit and then how he got the opportunity to study in the Bahamas. Even though Karamjit was living from hand to mouth, he was perceived to be some rich brat because of the watch he was wearing which seemed to be very expensive. And everybody who saw him with that watch on his wrists would literally believe that he is some super wealthy guy but in fact, he barely had any money left now. Nile was constantly chattering with his friends and Karamjit would just sit there sipping his coffee and listen to them talk.

They would ask for his opinion on some matters in the middle of the discussion but he would generally refrain from expressing his views on a specific topic. "Okay, I'll have to go now." " See you tomorrow Karamjit, Bye. And don't pay the bill. We'll pay it for you." " N0-N0. Why should you pay my bill? I'll pay it myself." "We are friends Karamjit. You don't have to worry about nothing. You just go. We'll pay for it. After all, we can pay just five bucks for our new friend huh?" he said jokingly.

Karamjit left and as soon as he went out of their sight, Nile began to talk to his friends about Karamjit. " Did you see that guys?" "What?" one of them asked. " This dude is super rich." Said Nile. " How do you know that?" " You klutz, didn't you see the watch he was wearing on his wrist? That tell you a whole lot more about him then he actually revealed." " So what?" someone said. " What do you mean 'so what'?" he continued. " I mean, he is a good funding source for our parties dude. He won't mind giving us some money for our bar parties. Don't you get it? We have got this one after a lot of time." " That's a good idea" someone said. " And this dude doesn't even have the courage to speak for himself so even if we take his money, he wouldn't dare to speak against that. I don't know whether I should be glad that I am gifted with a victim like him or feel sad for his ignorance that he cannot see his own good just because of the pressure of other people with him. This the worst thing that you could ever do to yourself i.e. to doubt yourself and allow others to dictate your life. Ha... Rich guy with a poor mind" said Nile as he laughed off.

When Karamjit met Nile the next day, Nile told him to go with them for a party. Karamjit as always tried to refuse but in the end, Nile took him along with him and his other friends. "Come with me Karamjit" said Nile as he sat on his bike. Karamjit sat on the back seat and Nile drove them through the narrow streets for five minutes until they reached the 'Pro Bar'. Karamjit although thought that it was not right for him to do this party stuff as he thought that it would be a kind of betrayal with the trust that his uncle placed on him before he came here. He could almost remember the words of his uncle striking his mind that he spoke to him that night. He couldn't waste his time in these unnecessary things but now he was already at the Bar so he found it absurd to resist at this moment.

He went along with Nile into the bar. This was his first time that he went in a bar. He knew that it was not right for him to do that and even his conscience stated to him that somehow it was not right to go with those people to the bar at such a time in evening but he still continued as it was too late for him to go back now. He saw the DJ playing the songs, dancers dancing on the jiggling dancing floor. While some of them were drinking beer and other drinks and talking. Nile took

Karamjit with him to the front bar and ordered a Standard. Karamjit didn't knew what a standard was. So he asked him , " What is a standard?"

"Standard? You don't know what a standard is?" Nile responded with an unusual surprised look. " Standard is the special beer in the Bahamas. When you open the bottle, smoke comes out of it. And boy, let me tell you, standard is the best that you can get in the Bahamas. It feels like you are drinking and smoking at the same time." "Back home, we have the famous Patiala Peg, but don't order for me, please. I don't drink" said Karamjit. " Are you kidding me dude? You don't drink? That's shocking. You haven't taken a drink ever before?" he asked. " I have tasted beer before but I am not a regular liquor drinker." " That's terrible man. So what do you want to eat. Order something for yourself." Karamjit resisted to drink or eat anything. " No, I am good man. Don't want to eat or drink anything. Thanks for asking" he said. " No-no. You have to have something. Let me order a coke for you." Nile pressurized him saying that.

Nile along with his friends started drinking, meanwhile, Karamjit was lost in the glamour and lighting of the bar as he looked around the bar and saw everywhere he looked that people were dressed up in a rather undignified manner which reflected to him a part of the culture that they have originated. Nile saw Karamjit sitting idle so he called him and asked him to drink the standard. " Karamjit just have a taste of the standard and you will ask for it again." " No, I have told you before that I don't drink" " Look, I am not asking you to drink the whole bottle . Just sip a little and feel its taste. Take it and be a man. You are not a kid anymore telling that you can't drink. At least taste it man." He said as he handed over the bottle of standard to Karamjit.

Karamjit took a sip out of it and felt its bitter taste. " Its good right? Drink some more of it" insisted Nile. Karamjit took some more of the standard and felt better drinking it. He continued to drink and Nile could see that it was now difficult for him to stop Karamjit from drinking it and he was successful in making him drunk. It was too late for Karamjit to realize that he had gone too far until he emptied the whole bottle. But he still didn't stop there. He asked Nile for another bottle. And Nile ordered it. After finishing the second bottle, Karamjit could take it no more and Nile could feel that he was completely wet with liquor and it was the right time to talk to Karamjit and let him reveal all his secrets without any effort from his part. He asked Karamjit to talk about his life at Patiala and his relationship with Riya.

Karamjit couldn't keep himself focused on anything. Instead his mind went back to Riya and that amazing last night of passionate sex. He eyed one of the dancers who seemed to be looking at him and smiled at her with a wanting stare. She winked at him. That was when he felt himself get aroused. He was in the right headspace to blow everything on alcohol and women. He missed Riya, and the best way to fix such painful yearning was to satisfy his male urges. He started breathing heavier and drinking more, drowning out the thoughts with anything he could. Nile sat back in disbelief, well aware he wasn't getting anything out Karamjit tonight. He was already gone. "You know what? We can just sit here and enjoy ourselves," he said.

"I'm not sittin' nowhere," said Karamjit.

And Karamjit had no sense of what he was talking about after drinking two bottles of standard which made him completely hypnotized releasing excess amounts of dopamine in his brain giving him pleasurable sensations. He tried to stand up but trembled and fell back on the ground again. Nile picked him up. " Ha-Ha-Ha. Looks like you have drank too much Karamjit. Two bottles of standard huh? It could make even the professionals drowsy, and this was the first time you drank. Ha-Ha-Ha" he laughed it off.

Karamjit went ahead to the dancers on the dancing floor and grabbed one of them and started dancing with them. It was something that he couldn't have imagined doing without getting wet with alcohol.

He approached the dancer just as she was stepping off the stage. "How much would it cost me to buy you a drink?" he asked her in a slurred voice.

She looked at him and smirked, knowing she found herself someone worthy of her time. "That depends on your tab," she said.

"I'll give you all I got," said Karamjit, clearly not thinking clearly. The woman walked with him to one of the booths in the back, giving him a chance to plead his case as he insisted on buying her a drink, calling over a waitress and sitting across from her. "So uh, tell me what you're into and I'll do it," he exclaimed. "I haven't planned on stopping yet so... what's your name?"

"Sherry," she said with a chuckle, finding him both laughably pathetic yet endearingly cute. "You seem funny. Maybe I would like to get to know you better." The dancer kicked off one of her heels and moved her naked foot slowly up Karamjit's leg as he could feel all the blood rushing to his dick as it immediately became erect. Karamjit's face of excited intrigue told Sherry all she needed to know as she smirked and moved her foot upwards. Karamjit felt it rub over his girthy meat as he looked down to see her beautiful painted toes softly caressing his package. Sherry chuckled. "You know, I really enjoy this type of casual conversation, Karamjit," she said slyly to him just as the waitress left. "Just don't mind under the table."

Karamjit breathed out slowly as he tried to form a coherent sentence. All he could think about was this woman's foot as it rubbed up on his dick with such eagerness. He was too drunk to question why she would be so interested, but it was clear she wasn't going to mince words about what she was willing to do for a payday. Her toes clenched around the formation of his shaft on his pants as she stroked it slowly. Karamjit said nothing but stared wide-eyed at her as the waitress returned and set down their drinks. Sherry used her toes to slowly unzip Karamjit's pants as he almost jumped in his seat. He startled the waitress as he quickly saved face. "Excuse me," he said. "I think this might be my last one."

Sherry grinned as she put her foot back into her heel and strapped it back up with a finger. "Why not save that drink and follow me," she said as she winked at him.

She stood up and strutted her way to the back of the building to the woman's bathroom. She watched to make sure Karamjit was looking as she motioned for him to follow her. Karamjit nodded and he casually made his way out of his seat, stumbling along the way. His heart was pounding with excitement as he was ready and willing to try out Sherry's kinky sales pitch, his body too drunk and horny to think of anything else. He quickly walked towards the bathroom and stood near the woman's door. He rubbed around his collar and cleared his throat only to see the door swing open and Sherry grab him by the lining of his pants and pull him into the small single person bathroom before anyone noticed.

"Sherry, was it? What are you-" Karamjit began to speak but Sherry was quick to press her hands firmly against his mouth and shush him. He looked around and realized it wasn't a bathroom at all, but a private room meant for personal dances. "A-are you about to give me a dance?"

She smirked a devilishly sly grin as her hand ran down the side of the door behind him and he could hear her lock it. Karamjit breathed out heavily as he watched her step back away from him and begin to sway her body sexually. "Something like this?" she whispered to him. She gestured again for him to keep quiet with a seductively little grin and wiggle of the shoulder before she slipped her hand down her navel and into her pants. She moved her skinny body like a wave in front of Karamjit as he found himself slowly reaching down and stroking his hard dick while staring at her. "Is this what you like?" she asked

"You're goddamn right it is," said Karamjit with a drunken hiccup as he watched with exhilaration.

Sherry bit her lip and nodded to him that she really wanted to see his piece. Karamjit breathed out and shrugged at this point. It had gone past the point of too far. He knew he was buying what she was selling before she did anything else. He slowly unzipped his pants as Sherry started noticeably rubbing herself with her hand down her panties. She moaned some as she watched Karamjit slowly pull his dick out of his boxer briefs. She gasped at the size, having not truly noticed before how big he felt. She licked her lips and nodded for him to start stroking it in front of her. Karamjit nodded as he rubbed his hands along his shaft in a slow motion for her to watch. His precum was already glistening on top of his head as Sherry took a step closer. She looked at Karamjit with a sly smile as she pulled her fingers up from her panties and sucked on them.

Karamjit watched as Sherry slowly undid the buttons of her dancer's blouse to reveal the black lingerie bra that left little to the imagination underneath. She pushed her hands up on her breasts for him to stare at and appreciate their softness. She leaned extra close to Karamjit to where he could feel her hot breath on his lips. She grabbed his hands and guided them to her chest as Karamjit was more than happy to take hold of her. As he did, Sherry kissed him hard and he slipped his hands under her bra and grasped a hold of her pointy, hard nipples. Sherry moaned into Karamjit's mouth as he squeezed her. She wrapped her arms around his neck and pulled him away from the door. The two walked back towards the counter of the restroom as Karamjit could feel his dick pressed against Sherry's bare stomach.

Sherry then pulled her arms back and leaned against the counter, her hands grasping Karamjit's dick tight. Karamjit clenched her breasts in surprise as he looked at her. Sherry wore a devious smile as she looked back at him before slowly going down on him. Karamjit gasped in exasperation as he felt Sherry's warm lips cup his head and suck off the salty sweet precum that had been milking out of him. Sherry grasped Karamjit's pants and boxers and swiftly pulled them down to reveal his full package. She grasped her hands firmly on his testicles as she dropped her head deeper down on his dick. Karamjit groaned at the amazing sensation. Her tongue caressed his rigid shaft as she explored up and down the entirety of his dick. She was on her feet, squatting so he could see how flexible she was as she mouth hugged his shaft with vigor.

Sherry sucked hard on Karamjit's dick. To the point he could hear her nearly gag herself as she went at it like a hungry animal getting overly excited about their first time. She caressed Karamjit's balls in her hand in such a way he could feel her milking his dick with more precum that she happily swallowed. Sherry started going harder still as she was getting serious. She pushed Karamjit back towards the wall as she thrusted his dick down her throat vigorously. She grasped the lower end of his shaft with her hand as she paid special attention to his upper half. Karamjit writhed some in the overload of sensations as he could feel himself drawing closer to an orgasm. He didn't want to cum immediately and potentially lose out on performing for this woman.

Karamjit made an attempt at moving Sherry up so he could take charge but she refused to budge from her position. Karamjit could see she was masturbating furiously through her pants with her free hand as the taste of his dick was more than enough for her. She gagged and deepthroated him as saliva dripped off his dick with each pull of her mouth. She used her hand on his dick to start twisting and using the lubrication to double the amount of pleasure that Karamjit felt. Karamjit practically danced in his shoes as he felt his whole body clenching up. He grasped at her hair and squeezed a ball of it in his hand, Sherry enjoyed the enthusiasm as she moaned on his dick. She could feel it throbbing from the sensations and reaching a point that it would overload. She stroked his dick as she felt the hot liquid shoot through his dick and into her mouth.

Karamjit watched in shock and awe as Sherry sucked hard on his dick to drink up his cum. He held back his desire to moan loudly as he watched her continue to stroke out over the last drop that she could lap up with her tongue. Her whole body arched as she gasped and moaned on to Karamjit's sore meat as she came hard in her panties to the point some of her juices dripped onto the bathroom floor. Karamjit gasped in surprise as he leaned back more against the wall. Sherry stood up slowly as she pulled her perfect breasts back into her bra and rebuttoned her blouse. Karamjit looked at her in shock and awe as she licked her lips and kissed him on the cheek.

"I-I can do more!" he insisted.

She raised a brow. "Do you have a condom?"

"I c-can get one!" he exclaimed.

The woman rubbed her hand against his chest and bit her lip. "You look like you've had a fair share of drinks," she said. "Why don't we both be a little irresponsible?"

She was like a devil whispering in his ear to do something he would regret. Of course, he had no filter to hold himself back from saying no. "I'll rock your world!" he exclaimed.

She licked her lips and turned around, pressing her hand to the wall and pulling down on her tights, exposing a perfectly shaped ass unlike anything Karamjit had seen before. She rubbed it and open herself up to him. "You can do me right in the backdoor entrance," she cooed with a very dirty look in her eye. "I'm clean."

Karamjit couldn't help but stare for a second but very swiftly obeyed as Sherry felt his hands grasp either side of her ass, before the length of his shaft entered her tight hole with ease as it had been properly lubed by her salvia. She had taken just about all she could manage but she knew that she had to let him finish. Not to mention the tenseness in her anus felt so good with his meat filling it. Harder and faster he pumped into her, working his dick in her tightness as carefully and indulgently as possible. Sherry arched her back and pushed herself backward, finding it easier in this position to meet his enthusiasm. Karamjit continued to pump, filling her once again to the point that there was nothing more she could concentrate on. With each pump now she could feel the throbbing of his dick hitting her from new angles. Each thrust Karamjit made, she made back, pushing just as hard and just as fast. He was about to climax again! She pushed against him with her hands on the wall and her ass bouncing off his body.

"I'm going to cum," he said as he clenched tight to her ass with his hands as he too finally felt his body begin to shake. "Ohh yeah, this is the best thing ever!"

Karamjit pumped harder and harder still, feeling himself on the edge, the breath in him rising and falling as he pounded harder and harder until suddenly the same warmth that Sherry had given him with her mouth suddenly rose up in him like a volcano about to explode. With that warmth came an overwhelming sense of pleasure for both of them. He thrusted into her as hard as he could, squeezing at her backside as suddenly the feeling of hot liquid shot forward from him, filling Sherry's insides with cum. She too arched back, gasping and grabbing at the cushions off the booth as the warmth of his semen fully awakened the pleasure in her once again. She arched her back and shot backward trembling, shaking on him just as he shook inside her, and with a final groan, Karamjit pulled backwards and watched as the cum slowly fell from her ass, over her throbbing pussy lips, and rolled down her thigh.

"Oh, my god," shouted Sherry with a cry as she fell forward, no longer able to hold herself up.

She gasped for air as her face met the pillow and Karamjit was quick to fall down beside her. The room felt like a sauna, both of them covered in sweat and struggling to catch their breath. And just like that, it ended. The beautiful Sherry thanked him and reminded him he will see this charged on his tab. Karamjit didn't care. He was far past that point of caring anymore. He was drunk and just experienced something so amazing he was afraid he'll forget it by the morning. He got himself back up and decided to head to the dance floor, pulling his pants up all the way as he stumbled out of the private room, ready for some more fun.

He continued dancing with all his passion until he became tired and fell back to the floor again. Nile asked him if they should leave now. Karamjit agreed. When the bill of their drinks and food came, Nile took off the wallet from Karamjit's pocket and handed over the money for the bill to the waiter. He then put his arms around Karamjit and took him to the cab and went off on his bike.

Karamjit was drunk so he couldn't speak clearly and it became difficult for the cab driver to know where he wanted to go. But somehow, he managed to drop him at his apartment. Karamjit stepped out of the cab completely drunk with his feet staggering while he was walking looking like he was almost about to break down in the middle of the street. He somehow gathered himself around to the apartment's main door.

"Knock, knock!" he shouted as he knocked at the door. " Open the door you old woman. Who do you think you are huh?" he shouted again. Mrs. Olsen heard his voice and she came out of her room to see who as at the door. As Mrs. Olsen opened the door and smelled the liquor out flowing from his mouth. She asked, " Are you drunk Karamjit?" " Noooooo. I am not." He said with his head shaking as he walked inside the apartment and continued walking straight to his room. " How dare you come drunk here? I told you the rules on the very first day you came here." She said. But Karamjit failed to listen to her and continued towards his room.

She didn't try to say anything to him further as she knew he wasn't in a position to listen to her so shouting at him at this moment would be a waste. He opened his room fell on the bed like a sack of potatoes without removing his shoes or changing his clothes. When he woke up the next morning, he realized that he had a pain in his back and his head was aching like someone banged it into a metal pole. He got up and looked in the mirror only to find that he hasn't changed his clothes. Then he reminded of the last night. He remembered that how he drank too much and then danced with the pub girls and came drank to Mrs. Olsen. He was extremely disappointed at what he did. He went downstairs to talk to Mrs. Olsen about the last night and apologized to her for what he did.

Mrs. Olsen was eating her breakfast when he came to her. " Mrs. Olsen.... Can I talk to you for a second please?" he asked. Mrs. Olsen stared at him but said not even a single word. He then continued, " Mrs. Olsen, I am extremely apologetic for coming drunk last night. I didn't want to drink but people that took me there forced me to drink and I couldn't resist them." " What?" she exclaimed. " You couldn't resist them? Oh come on, don't present such silly and pointless excuses to me. You mean, a grown up man like you couldn't resist them? You are acting like a kid now. Nobody could over rule you if you have a strong conviction to not do something that's against your values. I thought you must be knowing that by now, but no, I was completely wrong on that aspect." She said. " I am sorry for doing that Mrs. Olsen. I promise to never repeat that again." He said. "Since this is the first time you committed this act, you can get away with it. But I am warning you now for the last time, if you ever did that again in this house, I will throw you out. This is a holy house. We believe in the lord and we don't tolerate anyone who violates that holiness with their impure acts. Do you get it?" she asked. " I promise you that. Thanks for your generosity"

Karamjit changed his clothes and got ready to go to university and attend his lectures but when he opened his wallet, he found that he had lost about $100 from it. He was shocked. " Where is the money" he said in astonishment. He tried to remember realizing that while he was drunk someone might have taken it out. " Probably Nile took it to pay the bills?" He thought to himself. When he reached the university, he asked Nile about it and to his fear, it was true that Nile took off his money to pay the bills. He became absolutely annoyed at Nile.

" Why did you took my money? I didn't asked you to get me drinks. Did I?" " Relax, Karamjit. It was just $100 and that little money is grains of sand for you. Right? Of course, you are rich so you can spare that much money every day for your friends." Said Nile in a rather casual way. " Who told you that I am rich huh? I never told you that. Even if I were, why would I spend my money on your trivial habits of drinking?" he shouted. " Hey, hey, hey. Don't act so prejudice on me. Okay? The watch that you are wearing on your wrists tells anyone how rich you are. Don't try to hide that with the fabrication of your words." " But wearing this watch doesn't make me rich. How can you form an opinion about someone by just looking at how they dress or how they speak? That is pathetic. We're friends no more. Do you get the memo? It's over. You broke the trust, and I am getting out of here right away. Don't you speak to me ever again." Said Karamjit looking at Nile with his boiled up face. " Alright dude. Go away and don't show me your crying baby face again. Who do you think you are huh? You are nothing more than a complaining little boy. That's who you are." Said Nile. Karamjit left for his lecture and made a vow to himself to never talk to Nile again.

But it was not the end of the problem for him and his situation even worsened further. He was again left alone with no friends. As Nile was the one who actually influenced the whole group because of his persuasion skills and humor, he would tell everyone to not to talk to Nile and even bully him whenever they get the opportunity to do so. They would try to humiliate Karamjit when he was around their group with their jokes and they made sure that they could make life worse for Karamjit as he had nobody to defend for him. But Karamjit would simply not respond to them even though they continued with their misbehavior. He would listen to the lectures carefully and then come back home right away without messing with Nile and his friends who bullied him.

There was much lesser theoretical work for him now unlike school where he would have to read and read until he gets the concept. But here, there was much more focus on the practical functionality of things which made him like this system of education and eventually he started working hard on learning things which made it easier for him to get deeper into the concepts which the teachers taught him and grasp them with comprehension.

8.

The Turnaround....

Karamjit's life went on with him following his regular routine day after day. Days, weeks, months and then two years passed by and now he was in the final semester of his three years bachelor's degree completion after which it was time for him to go back to India. But he was worried that he hasn't yet fulfilled the last will of her mother of meeting Emmanuel Joshua. He got into the Bahamas but two years have went passed and he hasn't yet explored this archipelago. He didn't wanted to leave the Bahamas without finishing that. So he decided that once he finishes his final semester, he would surely take a trip and visit every place in the Bahamas and consequently try to find if that person is still alive or not.

One day, after he finished his economics lecture, the professor stopped him tapping on his shoulder. It was Professor Nathan. " Karamjit, I want to meet somebody. This is Professor Joshua. He is a Philosopher." He said as he pointed out to an old aged man probably in his seventies in a coat standing tall in front of him. Professor Nathan continued talking to Professor Joshua, " Professor, this is Karamjit. He is the student that I was talking about." " Oh I see, so you are the one that I have heard so many complements about, young man. I have heard him saying about you that you are a very sincere student and never miss his lectures. Well... I appreciate that." Said Professor Joshua. Karamjit looked at Prof. Joshua and thought to himself: Is it the person that I heard about from Uncle? " Thanks Professor for your kind comments. Can I know your full name please?" said Karamjit blushing out trying to confirm if he was the person he was looking for. "Sure, young man. I am Emmanuel Joshua. My students generally call me Prof. Joshua" he said. And it was at this moment that Karamjit realized that he was the exact person that he heard about. The Professor then continued, " So what are your future aspirations after completing your bachelor's degree, young man?" he asked. " I.... I am afraid I haven't thought about it yet, Professor." " Well, you must ponder over that for some time. We really need individuals like you who take life seriously. Trust me, the old man standing in front of you is 79 years old and most of the students that I have met until now in my life do not take life seriously. And what I have observed from my observation is that you are quite different from all of that majority out there. You have the potential to create something big and leave a mark in your areas of competence." He said as Karamjit stood there quietly listening to him speak.

" But the only issue that I see with you as pointed out by most of the people and probably you know that as well, is that you don't speak much. So unless you speak for yourself, nothing will change for you. Do you understand me?" he asked. And Karamjit nodded his head in agreement. "No you don't. I can't explain it to you in just two minutes what I have learned in two decades. Karamjit, I know that you want to live a bigger life than you are living now. I know that you have that deep desire in your heart to get out of your rut. So I want you to take some of your time and attend my class tomorrow after which I want you to clear any of your doubts or queries if you have any. But make sure that you attend tomorrow's class. And I promise you that I will completely change you into a person that you desire to be but haven't tried because of your insecurities. So meet me tomorrow for sure." Explained Professor Joshua. " Surely I will attend your class professor. Thanks for your advice" he said as he left thinking that he finally met the person he was searching for. Now, he would realize why his mother wanted him to meet that man.

The next day he was eagerly waiting to attend Professor Joshua's lecture and as soon as he finished attending his other lectures, he reached the memorial hall where Professor Joshua was supposed to give his lecture.

As he entered the room, he saw that the hall was packed with people. He was amazed with the number of people that were sitting there that it was difficult for him to find a seat in the front rows. So he moved up to the back rows and after searching hard and looking around for some time, he finally found a seat and sat there.

People were still moving in and out but he remained seated there not wanting to lose his seat to other person. The lecture was about to start in five minutes and Professor Joshua arrived with a little cylindrical box in his hand while everyone else sitting in the hall gave him a round of applause. Karamjit didn't knew much about Professor Joshua but the way he received a warm appraise from the audience, it seemed it him that he certainly had some great achievements under his belt. He had seen no other professor in his two years spent at the university being treated with such respect as he was receiving.

The Professor asked his assistant to close the door so that no one else could enter the hall after he had started his lecture. After glaring at the audience , he smiled a little and then began, " My friends, you might be wondering why I have brought this little cylindrical box with me today. And you might be trying to figure out what is inside this box. And I will certainly tell you that later on. I will do a little demonstration in front of you all so that you can easily grasp what I am trying to make you understand." He said. After which he opened up the lid of the cylindrical jar and took something which seemed to be grains to Karamjit because he was sitting too far away so he wasn't able to clearly perceive what the Professor picked up in his hands.

The Professor continued picking up some seeds from the jar. He took it in his palms and tried to show it to everyone else and then asked, " Can any one of you tell me what this is?" " A Seed" some one answered from the audience. "Well, how can you prove that to me? I mean, what made you come to a conclusion that what you see in my hand is a seed?" he asked. No one responded. And then he continued placing the seed back in the jar. " You see, that is the problem with all of us. Not particularly referring it to any specific person but all of us have been victims of this delusional perception of the reality in believing some things which are not true and that has led us to some circumstances under which we become distressed. But If we can mould the present perception into a completely different set of perceived notions, that could lead to much better results." He said and paused for a little while as he cleared his throat while someone from the audience asked him, "So Professor, what is the correct way of thinking that you are talking about?"

"Well, let me finish it. I am very careful with the selection of my words while I speak." He said. "You see, a fact is completely different from the Truth. A fact is simply the description of the present situation of a thing or a person while the truth is their ultimate reality which is what that thing was made to be. Now, let me explain that to you with an example. So, I asked you what you see in my hand. And not to my surprise, most of you had responded that you saw a seed. Now, those of you who said that are right. But what you have said is just the fact. The fact is that I had a seed in my hand. But the truth is that if you put that seed under a given set of stimuli to which it responds in a progressive way, you will see growth. Which if we talk in terms of a seed, then it requires soil, some moisture, sunlight and all these different things which then combine together to result in the growth of the seed to become a tree. But that is not the truth about the seed either. The seed that grows into a tree has fruits on it which further has seeds in it and those seeds further has got trees in them with fruits with seeds with trees with fruits with seeds and trees with fruit with seeds with trees and this process goes on. So you may say that the fact is that I have a seed in my hand. But that does not constitute the truth. The truth is that I have a complete forest in my hand. Now, I want you to think about what I have said so far for two minutes and then tell me what you have learned from this principle." He said as he grabbed the glass of water and continued to glare at the audience. Karamjit was thinking about that story too. It was going through his mind iteratively.

"Okay" the professor continued. " So can anyone of you tell me what is the lesson that you have learned following this principle?" he asked as everyone was scratching their heads. Then he said, " You see friends, this is what happens with most of us. All of us have the potential and the capability to become a tree but we never realize it until it's too late. Why? Because we are too busy looking at the facts that we never bother to find the truth about something. The fact about you may be completely unparallel to your reality, your truth. The fact may be that you are broke now, but that does not cancel the truth that you have a million dollars in the bank in the future. The fact may be that you are depressed, but that doesn't cancel the happy and joyful person that you are. The fact may be that you are living from hand to mouth but that does not nullify the truth that one day you are going to have so much that you are going to help other people get what they want to give it away. And I call it the seed principle. We all are like that seed. Everything that we are supposed to do is within us, but all we need to do is just put ourselves in the right environment. And that is the reason I am sharing this lesson with you. Right environment for you is the people who help you grow, books that nurture you, and friends that encourage you to push past your limitations and improve on your blind spots. Just think about what I have shared with you today. Heed it in your mind and never forget it. I hope you have learned something new from this lecture today other than your academic lectures which might give you the information but does not bring any transformation. Thanks for your time. I will see you all tomorrow." Said the professor as he quietly left the hall. As soon as he left, everyone rushed through the hall door to get out of the hall but kept sitting there pondering over what Professor Joshua taught.

He was curious to learn more from the Professor, so he went looking for him. He searched all around the campus but he found him nowhere, in the mess, conference hall, staff but he couldn't find him. In the end, he went to Professor Nathan and asked him about Professor Joshua. Prof. Nathan told him that he was in the library and that if he ever wanted to meet him, he should simply go to the library without a second thought because that is where he is most of the times. It was a kind of second home for him. He rushed immediately to the Library where he saw Professor Joshua sitting at the corner chair of the room reading a book of philosophy which was titled "Beyond Good and Evil" by Frederick Nietzsche. He went to him and whispered, "Hello Professor Joshua." The Prof. looked at him and a smile rubbed off his face. "Oh, hello Karamjit. Please sit down." He said. And all of sudden Karamjit felt a sense of significance about himself. He thought to himself: Professor remembers my name? Am I that important to him?

" Yes Karamjit, did you had any queries?" he asked. " Prof. I attended your lecture today and it was very insightful for me. I felt that the principle that you shared with me was particularly relatable to me." He said. " Oh yes, it is. It is relatable to every single person on this damn planet" " I don't know how to say it Prof. but I never asked this to anyone else before." "Please go ahead." The professor said as he leaned forward to listen to Karamjit with full attention. " Actually what you said was one hundred percent true. But how can I apply that in my own life? What is its practical utility? I mean, don't get me wrong. Whatever you said sounds really good but can you please tell me how it can transform me as a person?" he asked. " Well Karamjit, that's where more that 99% of the people are stuck. Everybody is born dumb, naked and stupid. But some people manifest their true abilities and potential while most of them don't. Because they learns this information, understands it but then do not apply it. It's just like a smoking doctor, metaphorically speaking. He knows that smoking is not good for his health, he understands it but then in the end doesn't apply it. And that is completely useless. It's as good as not conceiving the information or the knowledge at all. I have given this advice to many people, some of them used it for the betterment of the society and themselves while there were others who squandered it. I would just tell it very plainly to you. Associate yourself with the right people. It's very simple. If you are broke and you want some help, you don't go asking for help from a person who himself is broke. No! That's insanely stupid. You go to a person who has got plenty money or the one who can help you connect to a person that has got some money. Right? It's the same way here. If you associate with people who are highly ambitious towards their goals, you are going to be the same way. But if you are associating with people who just barely make through the day, you will be filled with the exact same type of vibes. So that was number one: To associate yourself with right people. Number two is to have faith in your abilities to take on any task and believe that you can just squeeze it. If you can conceive and believe something, then you can achieve it. I have seen it my life personally. It's all in your head. And number three which according to me is the most important; Always keep learning. You have a huge competitive edge over other people when you become an absolute learning machine. Michelangelo was still learning at age 87! Compare your age with his. You haven't even started living your life yet. And I realized that you have this quality of always learning the very first time I met you. That's why you are still listening and I am still speaking. Because as they say: the teacher appears when the student is ready to learn." He explained all this to Karamjit.

" But Prof. I have this insecurity because of the way I look and I always have this fear of being judged by other people. How do I get rid of it?" asked Karamjit. " Well, well, well. I can't explain that to you just by hammering it in your brain. But you will learn it. Okay, so tell me, do you play any sport?" " No. I haven't played any sports at the State or National level. I just used to play some chess online on my desktop computer and a little football with my father when he visited home. Other than that, I have never played sports soberly. I don't think I am good at sports either" he said as he dropped his head down looking at the ground. " How did you find that you were never good at sports? See, you need to let go off some things that happened in the past and continue to surge ahead from this point onwards. Make this your starting point. And as I said, don't look at the facts, but make your own reality by choosing the environment. I want you to pick up any sport which you like and start playing it. You said that you played chess and some football. Then go for it. I can get you into the junior team of our university. They will let you play and from there on, if you perform well, you can get into the senior team. It doesn't matter whether you perform well or poor, just play it and I will see the changes in you in the period of next one month. Okay?" he asked. " I will pick chess and football then." " Great. See, you after one month then." Said the Professor.

And following the advice from Prof. Joshua, he joined the chess club and also got into the football team. His daily routine was now staggered as he would first attend his lectures and then grind hard in the football ground with others. And then play chess in the university's chess club. He made some friends in the football team and playing football gave him the strength and the endurance and he grew much more stronger and agile at the end of the month while playing chess made him think about the situations strategically that were kind of new for him. All in all, doing these physically enduring games not only toughened him up physically but also improved his mindset and perception towards certain things.

He was just one month into it and there were significant changes to his personality which were visible to everyone. Karamjit was now much more confident than ever. He was a completely different person now. Earlier he would complain about things if they didn't went the way he planned them to be but now he would consider every drastic situation careful and analyze how he can reap the maximum benefit out of it. Earlier, he used to see problems as adversity, but now every problem that he encountered was an opportunity for him to grow and make himself better.

When he started playing football, he wasn't very agile and fast. He fell several times, injured his knees and legs but he didn't give in, in those times which made his conviction even more strong. He no longer saw failure as a detour but as an opportunity to learn something from it and use it as an incubator to create something out of it which had never been produced before.

Amrit and his uncle Gurtej Singh could feel the confidence in his voice whenever they talked to him now and they were completely surprised by the way Karamjit had gone through this transformation. And indeed, playing sports really proved to be a crucial factor for Karamjit which was really helping him in his personal development. Now, he could see things clearly which were cluttered before because of his stagnant mindset. He never knew that he had a good instinct at playing chess or whether he was just born to be good at it. He soon represented his university team in several tournaments, some of which he won while losing inothers. But all in all, he never considered failure to be his permanent address now. He would now also guide his juniors in learning the basics of chess and improving their games which consequently improved his performance as he got a much deeper understanding and subtleties of chess. He was progressing with every passing week in his chess career and getting victories quickly. He was amazed at himself watching his progress over this short period of time. Although he never got into the football senior team but he continued to play as he understood that it was way more important to be in the game and enjoy it rather than focusing on the results. This belief and revelation made him realize that life is the similar way. We don't necessarily have to reach a goal that we have established but to enjoy the journey that takes us through to that goal. That's very important!

After a month he met with Prof. Joshua as he had promised him. And Prof. Joshua could see the way sports has helped Karamjit bring the best in him. He could see the confidence with which he walked. He was no longer the guy who would walk around with his shoulders dropped and face to the ground. Now, he was walking upright, with stern confidence and a cheerful smile on his face. " Hello Prof. Joshua" he greeted the Professor. " Hello dear. You promised me to spend your spare time in sports and I can say I am already perceiving some changes in your personality. So tell me what you have learnt from chess and football?" he asked.

" Prof. Joshua, first of all I am extremely thankful to you for your advice which has completely changed my life. I am not the same person anymore which I was a few weeks before. Playing sports has completely turned my life upside down. Although, I have not changed drastically but I can certainly say that I have seen my life take a major turn from being unconfident to becoming comfortable in my own skin. Football taught me that failures are not the end point. It's just a small detour which one faces while moving towards a higher end goal. So I no longer get discouraged when I encounter difficulties and rather I embrace them and move forward learning some lessons from them which would certainly help me in my future course of life. And from chess, I have lately come to appreciate the power of planning. I never used to believe in planning. Rather, I always thought that one should always execute even if they are going through the motions. It has taught me that it's important to plan. It's important to plan first using all their intelligence but when it comes to really trying it out, only then the execution should be ruthless. But planning certainly makes you insulated from the unnecessary risks or choices that you might have to make in the execution of that plan. So this is what I learned" he explained everything in detail to Prof. Joshua.

"Well done Karamjit, I am proud of you my boy. I always feel amazed when some of my mentee heeds everything I say carefully and then take it to the next level. I must say that you are fully deserving of the time that I invested in you. So, you are about to graduate from the University of the Bahamas. What's next for you?" he asked.

" You know, professor when I was a kid, I had this desire of travelling all around the world. But as I grew up, people around me painted an image in my mind that was conflicting with my imagination. They taught me to settle for something less than I was capable of achieving. Even my uncle told me to just get a job, make a living and settle down and live a regular life just like most of the people does. They ingrained in my mind that I was a backward child who did not had the mental faculty or intelligence to learn things fast just like other kids do. And the predicament is that I believed them and after I met you and learned these lessons, I finally realized that it were those beliefs which actually overtook my life from my control and gave control to other people's opinions and even expectations of me. I slowly lost control over my choices and became a convict of the convictions of people around me. I couldn't trust my abilities to achieve what I wanted. I wasn't always a shy, introverted and klutz like that. Everyone that I met kept telling me that I was shy, that I speak less, that I am afraid to talk to strangers, that I was a no good nick. It was due to all of these beliefs that led me to where I went. But you have made me realize that I am not what they say I am, I am what I believe I am. I believe that this is the most important lesson that I have learned in my entire life, and if I were to sum it up, I would say that I was only limited to the beliefs that I had accepted. Once I changed the beliefs about myself, everything started to change for me. I became a quick learner, a good athlete and with your help I am still working on my communication skills. I can't be more thankful to you Prof. Joshua. You are the person who also mentored my mother Kulvir Kaur. She was mentored under your mentorship program. She might have known how you could help others realize their true potential and maybe that's why she told my father to let me meet you here. Thanks a ton for whatever you have done for me so far."

Prof. Joshua was listening to the complete narrative which Karamjit narrated to him. While Karamjit was narrating his whole story, Prof. Joshua couldn't help himself and tears rolled down his eyes. He said in a trembling voice, " Kulvir? Yes, I know her. She was such a bright young girl with big dreams and aspirations. She really wanted to make a difference. You know what Karamjit? There could be no better scenario for a mentor whose mentee says to him that the mentor changed his life. You and your mother have given me that privilege. This is the happiness which all the seven billion people living on this planet strive for but never realize it until it's too late. Your legacy is never in buildings or finishing projects. Your legacy is measured by your ability to build people. Your legacy is build when you help others realize their greatness. And I have got that privilege that I could serve your mother and you as well in my lifetime. That's two generations. There's nothing more fulfilling than that." He said as he calmed himself down.

He then continued, "When I was a young lad, I was just like you; aimless and confused. But I had a stroke of luck that I got a mentor that guided me to become the kind of person that I am today. His name was Charles Munro. He is no more today. I said him the exact words that you said to me today. He was the person that build the man you see in front of you today. And when he was on his deathbed, he told me that he wanted me to mentor people just like the way he did and help someone realize their true potential." He said as he somehow controlled himself.

" That's great." Said Karamjit as he put hands on Prof. Joshua's shoulders. "Are you okay?" he asked. " Yes, I am good. Just some emotional burst remembering my mentor and his teachings. But I want you to stay strong Karamjit and don't forget what you have learnt so far. See, there are people who are fast learners and learn without going through any repercussions but then there are those who learn the lessons the hard way. You are one of those people. I know, you have gone through some tough times, but believe me, the trouble will never end. Until you are breathing, you are going to face plenty, plenty, plenty troubles. So embrace them and take life head on." He said.

Prof. Joshua then took a piece of paper out of the magazine that he was reading. On it was the advertisement of a public speaking event that was about to happen in the Bahamas Institute of Business and Technology. He asked Karamjit to participate in that event that would help him to become even a much improved speaker. If he were the old Karamjit, he would have thought several times and considered the consequences of participating in the event but this new Karamjit accepted it immediately without even giving it a second thought.

He went to the event with all his preparation for the speech. The event took place in a large hall packed with audiences from various other universities. When his turn came, he went to the podium and as he walked towards the speaking dice to hold the Mic, he could see the large gathering of people sitting in front of him waiting for him to speak. He felt nervous at once and thought that people would make fun of him and he would lose his face in front of so many people if he couldn't deliver the speech in the right manner. It was difficult for him to still leave behind the old Karamjit and move on with his new identity.

He remembered what he had learned. He took a deep breath and started commencing his speech. After he went two minutes into the speech, his heart started to calm down and he got back to normal calm state. After he finished his speech, he received a loud applause and a few standing ovations. He wasn't expecting that his speech would go so well. It was effortless for him to deliver the speech so confidently in front of these many people. He never would have thought in his wildest imaginations that he would be doing the stuff that he was doing now and even help others learn it.

His happiness was out of the bounds when he gave that speech which made him even more confident and convicted to pursue his dreams. Now, he started to believe in his dream of travelling all around the world and meeting with people ending up inspiring them with his life. Now, he could see the good in everything that happened to him in the past. If he had not gone through the traumatic experience that he went through, he wouldn't have this beautiful testimony of how an individual could completely transform their life if they want to.

He would meet with Prof. Joshua every other day and they would discuss on how Karamjit could incorporate some more changes in his life to become more effective in his areas of competence. They would keep sitting for hours discussing about the lives of the people which influenced the people in their times and made a significant impact on the world before they died. Prof. Joshua made Karamjit read those people's lives and then ask him to tell three important lessons that he learned reading those people's biographies. Karamjit was all excited to learn from him whenever he got the opportunity to do so.

He would now focus less on his academic studies, rather he believed that he should be studying more about the events and people that would take him closer to his life's calling. And so he did that efficiently. He started reading more and more. Some days he would literally spend his whole time reading books and grasping people's lives through their stories some of which inspired him while he learned from the mistakes of other's lives and tried not to incorporate those in his own life. Every passing day, he was becoming a critical thinker and the more he read and studied people's lives, the more aware he was becoming about life and ways of dealing with people.

He would start attending seminars and conferences, listen to tapes and read books, even share some of the experiences of his own life with other people which made him a good storyteller. He was now bold and confident which made him a good choice for every event or conference that took place in the university. He would keenly participate in every event and give speeches that left a lasting impact on people.

He wouldn't just recite the speech like a robot, but he included stories and events from his life and the foolish mistakes that he made along the way mixed with his laughter that gave people that listened to him an experience that would retain in their memory forever. He would encourage others to share their life experiences and live a larger life than they are currently living. In essence, he was on the path to becoming a motivational speaker with exceptional communication skills and the ability to inspire people with his stories.

And all this was the result of constant hammering and learning process that he was undergoing under the guidance of his mentor Professor Joshua. And Prof. Joshua made sure that he don't let Karamjit to get back to his old life by getting back to his comfort zone, so he would constantly give him some task to do to keep him engaged whether that be some physical activity or some research paper to analyze and formulate his conclusions. He did this purposefully to expand his conscience to a much higher level. Professor Joshua didn't even let Karamjit to take a day off to relax himself. He believed that body is a slave to the mind.

He once explained to Karamjit that whenever a person starts to do a task which is beyond their comfort zone, there comes a point where their body would start giving them signals telling them to quit the process. But at that moment, once you ignore those signals and keeping moving towards the goal in spite of those signals, that is when you become a better version of yourself.

He explained this to Karamjit by giving him example of a marathon runner. He said that once a runner starts running a marathon, he starts off excited and energetic but once the marathon progresses, there comes a point where he starts feeling weary and tired and his mind tells him to quit the marathon and take some rest. But the true strength of the runner is measured when he beats that stage and continues to move forward despite the pain and suffering that he is temporarily going through. And after he passes that stage, there comes another stage where running feels like a walk in the park to him. And as long as the marathon continues, he goes through all these different motions which try to deter him from finishing the marathon, but once he endures all of these motions, he comes out victorious.

And then Prof. Joshua metaphorically used this story and told Karamjit that the same is true for any task that we try to do going past our comfort zone, your mind and body starts resisting it but once we get past that stage and continue to move forward, it is then that we realize our true ability to move forward. It is then that we can look back and enjoy those memories of not giving in to adversity, pain or fear taking our souls. He explained several parables to Karamjit which helped him get a better understanding and a new perspective to look at life. He was always grateful for the wonderful mentor that he got in the image of Prof. Joshua and he couldn't thank God enough for that.

9.
The Aftermath

Karamjit was now two weeks away from completing his graduation and was ready to leave back to India back again. He was sitting in his apartment studying some research papers while he got a call from Prof. Joshua who called him to the university and said him to come immediately stating the matter to be urgent. Karamjit immediately went to the campus and met the professor who was talking to another person dressed up in a coat with his slow shine shoes reflecting everything holding a suitcase in his hand.

"Yes professor" said Karamjit as he stood close to him. "Karamjit meet Mr. Ashton, he is the managing director of one of the largest executive consultation firms in America. He provides training for people who would then become executive coaches for businesses and individual leaders to help them maximize their performance in their organizations." Said Prof. Joshua. Karamjit greeted Mr. Ashton shaking hands with him.

"He is looking forward to take some of the students from this university and give them a free internship and train them to train leaders in the organizations strategically and emotionally to help them make better decisions and run the organization following a better performance driven approach." He explained. " Oh... I see." Said Karamjit. "And I have recommended your name to him. He is leaving after three weeks and by that time, you would have acquired your bachelor's degree. So you can go with him to America and learn more about business consultancy." Said Prof. Joshua. "Uhh... Professor, can I talk to you for a second please? Just you and me." Karamjit whispered in his ears. " Sure. Excuse us Mr. Ashton. Please go around and take a look at the university campus until we meet in the evening" he said as he walked away with Karamjit.

" Yes tell me what you want to say" he asked him. " Professor you haven't asked me about that before. I can't go with Mr. Ashton to America, I am about to finish my course and I have to return to India after that." " Look, this is a lifetime opportunity that you are getting offered. Many students look forward to join their consultation firms and you are getting to join it for free with my recommendation. You should utilize it, that's all I would say to you. Take your time to consider this opportunity and tell me when you have made your mind. And make sure that you make a decision that can make your mother proud for you. It's an important decision so take your time and let me know by tomorrow evening because I have to make the final list of students who will be going there. And remember, make a decision so that your future self can look back at you and say- 'I am glad that you made that choice'" said Professor Joshua glaring at Karamjit as he left him quietly without further saying anything.

Karamjit went back home and he couldn't sleep the whole night thinking of what Prof. Joshua told him. He felt like calling Amrit and ask him to help him make a decision but he realized that it was he who has to make the choice.

He decided to call up Riya to help make up his mind about the offer he received. Oh how good it felt to hear her voice again. Whereas before Karamjit would have started small talk and end up awkwardly bumbling through his words trying to talk to her, now he felt like he could be assertive with how much he missed her. He told her that a lot has happened but now, more than ever, he could use her right now. She said the same, and then there was the trigger. The sweet sound of her voice. It made Karamjit feel wild. She wasn't there though. That didn't mean they could have a little private fun. He told her he wanted her to close her eyes and listen to the words he spoke. He was confident enough in his newfound skills that he could satisfy her on fantasy alone. Riya was unsure what he was going for, but her own longing made it impossible to say no to the thought of phone sex.

"Just listen to how I describe it and touch yourself," he whispered to her. "I will do the same. The fantasy will bring us together, no matter how far apart we are."

"Tell me," she whispered.

"I want you to imagine me between your legs," he whispered. "Holding you by the ankles." A man who was always looking for some sort of control would of course be into some kind of hot and erotic kinks, but to be able to make her feel like he was really there with his words showed he was something much more. He whispered more. "I then crawl over you onto the bed. You feel my body heat over you." She listened to him as he started kissing softly on her stomach, moving upwards over her breasts. "I lightly kiss your nipples..." he spoke softly. She clinched her toes in pleasure. It was as if he was there. "I gently rub my fingers over your lips."

"And I suck on them seductively," she cooed back at him. "I then take those fingers and move them down my body."

He smirked. "I lubricate myself with your juices as courtesy before I slide into you," he said. "I fill you up with all of my love and cradle you on the bed."

Riya gasped as the thought of Karamjit filling her up. She moaned heavily in exasperated pleasure, wanting badly to reach around and hold him by the neck. She refrained, not wanting to break the illusion of him not really being there. Karamjit smirked and breathed out heavily as he started telling her more. "I am now thrusting deep into you," he said. "I continue to kiss along your neck and breasts, enjoying every moment of tasting your fine, tender skin. Our hips grind against each other as I slowly reach around and grab that fine, firm ass." She felt all of the overwhelming sensations encompassing her all at once. "From my shaft thrusting inside of you to the soft, romantic kisses on your body. My hands ravenously search for every single piece of you to touch."

For several minutes, the two talked like they were staring into each other's eyes as they made passionate love. It was clear Karamjit was getting a lot of pent up energy out of his system with Riya. He had always stared at her longingly, enough so that he could easily see her before him. He touched himself to the rhythm of her moans and it felt like she was riding him. She bit her lip. "I pull myself up, kissing you again like it was the last time all over again," she said.

They both started to convulse from the overload of orgasmic sensations. Their bodies stiffened as Riya could barely breathe from the amount of buildup. She let it all out in a single, long winded exhale of pleasure as she climaxed, shaking wildly on her bed. Karamjit moaned with her as he moved his body and in a steady and slow, rhythmic motion to orgasm into some tissue. "I pet your hair gently, praising you with these hands of mine," he said softly. She could sense nothing but pleasure and the strong smell of sweat in his hair. A memory of their last time together coming back. It was an intoxicating rush that brought her to a full climax. "I then kiss you again and remind you how much I love you..."

After the intense phone sex, both of the lovers missed each other even more. Karamjit was satisfied with himself and what he had done for her. With the passions out of the way, he moved the conversation towards why he originally called, letting Riya share with him her thoughts. Overall, the night was an overwhelming experience, and in the end he came out a better man.

He knew that he can no longer depend on people he trust to make life's decisions for him. The next day he met Prof. Joshua and told him that he was ready to go with Mr. Ashton to learn consultancy. Prof. Joshua was happy and excited for Karamjit. He hugged Karamjit almost immediately when he told him that he was ready. Karamjit called his uncle Gurtej Singh and told him about the matter. He told him that he cannot visit India as he'll have to go to America to learn management consultancy. He was expecting resentment from his uncle but instead his uncle happily told him that he was free to do what he had decided to do with his life. Maybe it was due to the changes that were ingrained in Karamjit that he reflected in the way he communicated his ideas. Karamjit was happy knowing that his uncle was rather excited about it

He called Amrit too and informed him about this golden opportunity that he had got. Amrit was happy for Karamjit. As they continued to talk, Karamjit came to know that Amrit is also about to complete his bachelor's degree in India and was looking forward to go abroad and find a job in some country. Karamjit advised him to work on his skills that could help him fetch some work in India only. He explained to Amrit how he got transformed completely and the things that helped him became the kind of person that he is today.

But Amrit had made his mind to live in another country instead of working on himself to add some value to himself by working on his skill set. Karamjit tried his mighty best to explain Amrit that he could live a contended life even if he lives in India and that going to some other country just for the sake of getting a job is not a good idea according to him but Amrit was stern on his decision. So, Karamjit made no further effort to get him to change his mind. He bid him goodbye and hung the call.

Karamjit also realized that all of what happened, has happened for his good as with the opportunity to be a management consultant also came the opportunity to travel another country. He came back to his apartment, arranged his clothes and his possessions, and put them together in his bag. He opened the window of his room to breathe some fresh air as his eyes looked up on to the sky. He was anticipating some adventure on his visit to America with some challenges which he looked forward to fight with un-daunting courage and perseverance. He was now ready to live a new chapter in his life with a glare of hope reflecting in his eyes. As he glanced down on his watch he knew it was time.

Don't miss out!

Visit the website below and you can sign up to receive emails whenever Gaganjeet Gujral publishes a new book. There's no charge and no obligation.

https://books2read.com/r/B-A-CMYN-UWGPB

BOOKS 2 READ

Connecting independent readers to independent writers.

About the Author

Education

Schooling : La Martinere for Boys, Kolkata

Graduation : Les Roches, Switzerland

Post Graduation: Indian institute of Management, Ranchi (IIM-R)

Vocation: Watchmaking / Founder of Hungerford.watch

I spent my college days in the mountains of switzerland in a Hotel school, but deep down in my heart my passion for writing was not encouraged at that time, although I wish it was since I would have then published my first book quite earlier.

Only recently after completing my MBA did i give my skill a go at it, after much encouragement from a beloved professor.

While spending time In my home office when my wife came to me and encouraged me to honour this gifted skill and share it with the world. I finally decided to publish a masterpiece for the readers.

Read more at https://www.hungerford.watch/.

www.ingramcontent.com/pod-product-compliance
Ingram Content Group UK Ltd.
Pitfield, Milton Keynes, MK11 3LW, UK
UKHW021657190726
13853UKWH00001B/313